SNOWBOUND WITH HIS INNOCENT TEMPTATION

BY
CATHY WILLIAMS

MILLS & BOON

First Published in Great Britain 2016
By Mills & Boon, an imprint of HarperCollins*Publishers*
1 London Bridge Street, London, SE1 9GF

© 2016 Cathy Williams

ISBN: 978-0-263-91656-0

e and recyclable
orests. The logging
vironmental

Short of throwing Theo to his fate in the driving snow outside, Becky had no choice but to put him up— and from the looks of the weather he was going to be around for at least another night.

Just the two of them under the one roof.

Becky's mind broke its leash and raced off in all sorts of crazy directions.

He was awful, with his generalisations and his sneering, patronising assertions, and that typical rich man's belief that money was the only thing that mattered…that he could just buy things and buy people…

In short, he was just the sort of guy she had no time for.

But he was so outrageously beautiful. And that was what gripped her imagination and held it. That was what shot through her head with the treacherous accuracy of a heat-guided missile, cutting a swathe through all logic and common sense…

This gloriously, sinfully beautiful man was going to be under her roof, and her whole body tingled at the thought of that.

Which was worse than crazy.

Cathy Williams can remember reading Mills & Boon books as a teenager, and now that she is writing them she remains an avid fan. For her, there is nothing like creating romantic stories and engaging plots, and each and every book is a new adventure. Cathy lives in London, and her three daughters—Charlotte, Olivia and Emma—have always been, and continue to be, the greatest inspirations in her life.

Books by Cathy Williams

Mills & Boon Modern Romance

A Virgin for Vasquez
Seduced into Her Boss's Service
The Wedding Night Debt
A Pawn in the Playboy's Game
At Her Boss's Pleasure
The Real Romero
To Sin with the Tycoon
The Uncompromising Italian
The Argentinian's Demand
Secrets of a Ruthless Tycoon
Enthralled by Moretti
His Temporary Mistress
A Deal with Di Capua
The Secret Casella Baby
The Notorious Gabriel Diaz

The Italian Titans

Wearing the De Angelis Ring
The Surprise De Angelis Baby

One Night With Consequences

Bound by the Billionaire's Baby

Visit the Author Profile page at
millsandboon.co.uk for more titles.

SNOWBOUND
WITH HIS
INNOCENT
TEMPTATION

To my three wonderful daughters

CHAPTER ONE

'HONESTLY, ALI, I'M FINE!' Complete lie. Becky Shaw was far from fine.

Her job was on the line. The veterinary practice where she had been working for the last three years was in the process of being sold—and being turned into yet another quaint coffee shop to attract the onslaught of tourists who arrived punctually every spring and summer, snapping the gorgeous Cotswold scenery with their expensive cameras and buying up all the local art in a flurry of enthusiasm to take away a little bit of local flavour with them. Her friends Sarah and Delilah had got it right when they had decided to turn their cottage into a gallery and workshop. Not that they had had to in the end, considering they had both been swept off their feet by billionaires.

And then there was the roof, which had decided that it was no longer going to play ball and she was sure that right now, if she listened hard enough, she would be able to hear the unnerving sound of the steady leak drip-dripping its way into the bucket she had strategically placed in the corridor upstairs.

'I keep telling you that you're too young to be buried out there in the middle of nowhere! Why don't you come out to France? Visit us for a couple of weeks? Surely the practice can spare you for a fortnight...'

In three months' time, Becky thought glumly, the practice would be able to spare her for approximately the rest of her life.

Though there was no way that she was going to tell her sister this. Nor did she have any intention of going out to the south of France to see Alice and her husband, Freddy. Her heart squeezed tightly as it did every time she thought of Freddy and she forced herself to answer her sister lightly, voice betraying nothing.

'I'm hardly *buried out here*, Alice.'

'I've seen the weather reports, Becks. I always check what the weather's doing on my phone and the Cotswolds is due heavy snow by the weekend. You're going to be trapped there in the middle of March, when the rest of the country is looking forward to spring, for goodness' sake! *I worry about you.*'

'You mustn't.' She glanced out of the window and wondered how it was that she was still here, still in the family home, when this was supposed to have been a temporary retreat, somewhere to lick her wounds before carrying on with her life. That had been three years ago. Since then, in a fit of lethargy, she had accepted the job offer at the local vet's and persuaded her parents to put all plans to sell the cottage on hold. Just for a little while. Just until she got her act together. She would pay them a monthly rent and, once she'd got herself on a career ladder, she would leave the Cotswolds and head down to London.

And now here she was, with unemployment staring her in the face and a house that would have to be sold sooner rather than later because, with each day that passed, it became just a little more run down. How long before the small leak in the roof expanded into a full scale, no-holds-barred deluge? Did she really want to wake up in the middle of the night with her bed floating?

So far, she hadn't mentioned the problems with the house to her parents, who had left for France five years previously, shortly having been joined by Alice and her husband. She knew that if she did the entire family would up sticks and arrive on her doorstep with tea, sympathy and rescue plans afoot.

She didn't need rescuing.

She was an excellent vet. She would have a brilliant recommendation from Norman, the elderly family man who owned the practice and was now selling to emigrate to the other side of the world. She would be able to find work somewhere else without any problem at all.

And besides, twenty-seven-year-old women did not need rescuing. Least of all by their younger sibling and two frantically worried parents.

'Shouldn't *I* be the one worrying about *you*?'

'Because you're three years older?'

Becky heard that wonderful, tinkling laugh and pictured her beautiful, charming sister sitting in their glamorous French gîte with her legs tucked under her and her long, blonde hair tumbling over one shoulder.

Freddy would be doing something useful in the kitchen. Despite the fact that he, like her, was a hard-working vet, he enjoyed nothing more than getting back from the practice in which he was a partner, kicking off his shoes and relaxing with Alice in the kitchen, where he would usually be the one concocting the meals, because he was an excellent cook.

And he adored Alice. He had been swept off his feet from the very first second he had been introduced to her. At the time, she had been a high-flying model on the way to greatness and, whilst Becky would never have believed that Freddy—earnest and usually knee-deep in text books—could ever be attracted to her sister—who was cheerfully proud of her lack of academic success and hadn't read a book cover to cover in years—she had been proved wrong.

They were the most happily married couple anyone could have hoped to find.

'I'll be fine.' Becky decided to put off all awkward conversations about job losses and collapsing roofs for another day. 'I won't venture out in the middle of a snow-storm in my pyjamas, and if anyone out there is stupid enough to brave this weather on the lookout for what they can nick then they won't be heading for Lavender Cot-tage.' She eyed the tired décor in the kitchen and couldn't help grinning. 'Everyone in the village knows that I keep all my valuables in a bank vault.'

Old clothes, mud-stained wellies, tool kit for the hun-dreds of things that kept going wrong in the house, envi-able selection of winter-woolly hats...just the sort of stuff any robber worth his salt would want to steal.

'I just thought, Becks, that you might venture out here and have a little fun for a while before summer comes and all those ghastly crowds. I know you came over for Christmas, but it was all so busy out here, what with Mum and Dad inviting every single friend over for drinks every single evening. I...I feel like I haven't seen you for absolutely ages! I mean, just the two of us, the way it used to be when we were younger and...well... Freddy and I...'

'I'm incredibly busy just at the moment, Ali. You know how it is around this time of year with the lamb-ing season nearly on us, pregnant sheep in distress ev-erywhere you look... But I'll come out as soon as I can. I promise.'

She didn't want to talk about Freddy, the guy she had

met at university, the guy she had fallen head over heels in love with, had he only known, the guy who had turned her into a good friend, who had met Alice, been smitten in the space of seconds and proposed in record time.

The guy who had broken her heart.

'Darling, Freddy and I have something to tell you and we would much rather tell you face to face…'

'What? What is it?' Filled with sudden consternation, Becky sat up, mind crash-banging into worst case scenarios.

'We're going to have a baby! Isn't it exciting?'

Yes, it was. Exciting, thrilling and something her sister had been talking about from the moment she had said *I do* and glided up the aisle with a band of gold on her finger.

Becky was thrilled for her. She really was. But, as she settled down for one of the rare Saturday nights when she wasn't going to be on call, she suddenly felt the weight of the choices she had made over the years bearing down on her.

Where were the clubs she should be enjoying? Where was the breathless falling in and out of love? The men in pursuit? The thrilling text messages? When Freddy had hitched his wagon to her sister, Becky had turned her back on love. Unlike Alice, she had spent her teens with her head in books. She'd always known what she'd wanted to be and her parents had encouraged her in her studies. Both were teachers, her father a lecturer, her mother a maths teacher at the local secondary school. She had always been the good girl who worked hard. Beautiful, leggy Alice had decided from an early age that academics were not for her and of course her parents—liberal, left wing and proud of their political correctness—had not batted an eyelid.

And so, while Becky had studied, Alice had partied.

'Everyone should be free to express themselves without being boxed into trying to live up or live down to other people's expectations!' had been her mother's motto.

At the age of eighteen, Becky had surfaced, startled and blinking, to university life with all its glorious freedom and had realised that a life of study had not prepared her for late-night drinking, skipping lectures and sleeping around.

She had not been conditioned to enjoy the freedom at her disposal, and had almost immediately developed a crush on Freddy, who had been in her year, studying veterinary science like her.

He, too, had spent his adolescence working hard. He, too, had had his head buried in text books between the ages of twelve and eighteen. He had been her soul mate and she had enjoyed his company, but had been far too shy to take it to another level, and had been prepared to bide her time until the inevitable happened.

Only ever having watched her sister from the sidelines, laughing and amused at the way Alice fell in and out of love, she had lacked the confidence to make the first move.

And in the end, thank goodness, because, had she done so, then she would have been roundly rejected. The boy she had considered her soul mate, the boy she had fancied herself spending her life with, had not been interested in her as anything but a pal. She had thought him perfect for her. Steady, hard-working, considerate, feet planted firmly on the ground...

He, on the other hand, had not been looking for a woman who shared those qualities.

He had wanted frothy and vivacious. He had wanted someone who shoved his books aside and sat on his lap.

He had wanted tall and blonde and beautiful, not small, dark-haired and plump. He hadn't wanted earnest.

As the dark night began to shed its first flurries of snow, Becky wondered whether retreating to the Cotswolds had been a good idea. She could see herself in the same place, doing the same thing, in ten years' time. Her kid sister felt sorry for her. Without even realising it, she was becoming a charity case, the sort of person the world *pitied*.

The house was falling down.

She was going to be jobless in a matter of months.

She would be forced to do something about her life, leave the security of the countryside, join the busy tide of bright young things in a city somewhere.

She would have to climb back on the horse and start dating again.

She felt giddy when she thought about it.

But think about it she did, and she only stopped when she heard the sharp buzz of the doorbell, and for once didn't mind having her precious downtime invaded by someone needing her help with a sick animal. In fact, she would have welcomed just about anything that promised to divert her thoughts from the grim road they were hell-bent on travelling.

She headed for the door, grabbing her vet's bag on the way, as well as her thick, warm, waterproof jacket, which was essential in this part of the world.

She pulled open the door with one foot in a boot, woolly hat yanked down over her ears and her car keys shoved in her coat pocket.

Eyes down as she reached for her bag, the first things she noticed were the shoes. They didn't belong to a farmer. They were made of soft, tan leather, which was already beginning to show the discolouration from the snow collecting outside.

Then she took in the trousers.

Expensive. Pale grey, wool. Utterly impractical. She was barely aware of her eyes travelling upwards, doing an unconscious inventory of her unexpected caller, registering the expensive black cashmere coat, the way it fell open, unbuttoned, revealing a fine woollen jumper that encased a body that was…so unashamedly *masculine* that for a few seconds her breath hitched in her throat.

'Plan on finishing the visual inspection any time soon? Because I'm getting soaked out here.'

Becky's eyes flicked up and all at once she was gripped by the most unusual sensation, a mixture of dry-mouthed speechlessness and heated embarrassment.

For a few seconds, she literally couldn't speak as she stared, wide-eyed, at the most staggeringly good-looking guy she had ever seen in her life.

Black hair, slightly long, had been blown back from a face that was pure, chiselled perfection. Silver-grey eyes, fringed with dramatically long, thick, dark lashes, were staring right back at her.

Mortified, Becky leapt into action. 'Give me two seconds,' she said breathlessly. She crammed her foot into wellie number two and wondered whether she would need her handbag. Probably not. She didn't recognise the man and, from the way he was dressed, he wasn't into livestock so there would be no sheep having trouble giving birth.

Which probably meant that he was one of those rich townies who had second homes somewhere in one of the picturesque villages. He'd probably descended for a weekend with a party of similarly poorly equipped friends, domestic pets in tow, and one of the pets had got itself into a spot of bother.

It happened. These people never seemed to realise that dogs and cats, accustomed to feather beds and grooming parlours, went crazy the second they were introduced to the big, bad world of the real countryside.

Then when their precious little pets returned to base camp, limping and bleeding, their owners didn't have a clue what to do. Becky couldn't count the number of times she had been called out to deal with weeping and wailing owners of some poor cat or dog that had suffered nothing more tragic than a cut on its paw.

In fairness, *this* man didn't strike Becky as the sort to indulge in dramatics, not judging from the cool, impatient look in those silver-grey eyes that had swept dismissively over her, but who knew?

'Right!' She stepped back, putting some distance between herself and the disconcerting presence by the door. The flurries of snow were turning into a blizzard. 'If we don't leave in five seconds, then it's going to be all hell getting back here! Where's your car? I'll follow you.'

'Follow me? Why would you want to follow me?'

His voice, Becky thought distractedly, matched his face. Deep, seductive, disturbing and very, very bad for one's peace of mind.

'Who *are* you?' She looked at him narrowly and her heart picked up pace. He absolutely towered over her.

'Ah. Introductions. Now we're getting somewhere. You only have to invite me in and normality can be resumed without further delay.'

Because this sure as hell wasn't normal.

Theo Rushing had just spent the past four-and-a-half hours in second gear, manoeuvring ridiculously narrow streets in increasingly inhospitable weather conditions, and cursing himself for actually thinking that it would be a good idea to get in his car and deal with this mission himself, instead of doing the sensible thing and handing it over to one of his employees to sort out.

But this trip had been a personal matter and he hadn't wanted to delegate.

In fact, what he wanted was very simple. The cottage into which he had yet to be invited.

He anticipated getting it without too much effort. After all, he had money and, from what his sources had told him, the cottage—deep in the heart of the Cotswolds and far from anything anyone could loosely describe as civilisation—was still owned by the couple who had originally bought it, which, as far as Theo was concerned, was a miracle in itself. How long could one family live somewhere where the only view was of uninterrupted countryside and the only possible downtime activity would be tramping over open fields? It worked for him, though, because said couple would surely be contemplating retirement to somewhere less remote...

The only matter for debate would be the price.

But he wanted the cottage, and he was going to get it, because it was the only thing he could think of that would put some of the vitality back into his mother's life.

Of course, on the list of priorities, the cottage was way down below her overriding ambition to see him married off, an ambition that had reached an all-time high ever since her stroke several months ago.

But that was never going to happen. He had seen first-hand the way love could destroy. He had watched his mother retreat from life when her husband, his father, had been killed suddenly and without warning when they should have been enjoying the bliss of looking towards their future, the young, energetic couple with their only child. Theo had only been seven at the time but he'd been sharp enough to work out that, had his mother not invested her entire life, the whole essence of her being, in that fragile thing called love, then she wouldn't have spent the following decades living half a life.

So the magic and power of love was something he could quite happily do without, thanks very much. It was a slice of realism his mother stoutly refused to contemplate and Theo had given up trying to persuade her into seeing his point of view. If she wanted to cling to unrealistic fantasies about him bumping into the perfect woman, then so be it. His only concession was that he would no longer introduce her to any of his imperfect women who, he knew from experience, never managed to pull away from the starting block as far as his mother was concerned.

Which just left the cottage.

Lavender Cottage...his parents' first home...the place where he had been conceived...and the house his mother had fled when his father had had his fatal accident. Fog...a lorry going over the speed limit... His father on his bicycle hadn't stood a chance...

Marita Rushing had been turned into a youthful widow and she had never recovered. No one had ever stood a chance against the perfect ghost of his father. She was still a beautiful woman but when you looked at her you didn't see the huge dark eyes or the dramatic black hair... When you looked at her all you saw was the sadness of a life dedicated to memories.

And recently she had wanted to return to the place where those memories resided.

Nostalgia, in the wake of her premature stroke, had become her faithful companion and she wanted finally to come to terms with the past and embrace it. Returning to the cottage, he had gathered, was an essential part of that therapy.

Right now, she was in Italy, and had been for the past six weeks, visiting her sister. Reminiscing about the cottage, about her desire to return there to live out her final days, had been replaced by disturbing insinuations that she might just return to Italy and call it quits with England.

'You're barely ever in the country,' she had grumbled a couple of weeks earlier, which was something Theo had not been able to refute. 'And when you are, well, what am I but the ageing mother you are duty-bound to visit? It's not as though there will ever be a daughter-in-law for me, or grandchildren, or any of those things a woman of my age should be looking forward to. What is the point of my being in London, Theo? I would see the same amount of you if I lived in Timbuktu.'

Theo loved his mother, but he could not promise a wife he had no intention of acquiring or grandchildren that didn't feature in his future.

If he honestly thought that she would be happy in Italy, then he would have encouraged her to stay on at the villa he had bought for her six years previously, but she had lived far too long away from the small village in which she had grown up and where her sister now lived. After two weeks, she would always return to London, relieved to be back and full of tales of Flora's exasperating bossiness.

Right now, she was recuperating, so Flora was full of tender, loving care. However, should his mother decide to turn her stay there into a permanent situation, then Flora would soon become the chivvying older sister who drove his mother crazy.

'Why are you getting dressed?' Theo asked the cottage's present resident in bemusement. She was small and round but he still found himself being distracted by the pure clarity of her turquoise eyes and her flawless complexion. Healthy living, he thought absently, staring down at her. 'And you still haven't told me who you are.'

'I don't think this is the time to start making chit chat.' Becky blinked and made a concerted effort to gather her wits because he was just another hapless tourist in need of her services. It was getting colder and colder in the little hallway and the snow was becoming thicker and thicker. 'I'll come with you but you'll have to drive me back.' She swerved past him, out into the little gravelled circular courtyard, and gaped at the racing-red Ferrari parked at a jaunty angle, as though he had swung recklessly into her drive and screeched to a racing driver's halt. 'Don't tell me that you came here in *that*!'

Theo swung round. She had zipped past him like a pocket rocket and now she was glaring, hands on her hips, woolly hat almost covering her eyes.

And he had no idea what the hell was going on. He felt like he needed to rewind the conversation and start again in a more normal fashion, because he'd obviously missed a few crucial links in the chain.

'Come again?' was all he could find to say, the man who was never lost for words, the man who could speak volumes with a single glance, a man who could close impossible deals with the right vocabulary.

'Are you *completely mad*?' Becky breathed an inward sigh of relief because she felt safer being the angry, disapproving vet, concerned for her safety in nasty weather conditions, and impatient with some expensive, arrogant guy who was clueless about the Cotswolds. 'There's no way I'm getting into that thing with you! And I can't believe you actually thought that driving all the way out here to get me was a good idea! Don't you people know anything *at all*? Not that you have to be a genius to work out that these un-gritted roads are *lethal* for silly little cars like that!'

'*Silly little car?*'

'*I'd* find the roads difficult and *I* drive a *sensible* car!'

'That *silly little car* happens to be a top-end Ferrari that cost more than you probably earn in a year!' Theo raked fingers frustratedly through his hair. 'And I have no bloody idea why we're standing out here in a blizzard having a chat about cars!'

'Well, how the heck are we supposed to get to your animal if we don't drive there? Unless you've got a helicopter stashed away somewhere? Have you?'

'Animal? What animal?'

'Your *cat*!'

'I don't have a cat! Why would I have a cat? Why would I have any sort of animal, and what would lead you to think that I had?'

'You mean you haven't come to get me out to tend to an animal?'

'You're a vet.' The weathered bag, the layers of warm, outdoor clothing, the wellies for tramping through mud. All made sense now.

Theo had come to the cottage to have a look, to stake his claim and to ascertain how much he would pay for the place. As little as possible, had been his way of thinking. It had been bought at a bargain-basement price from his mother, who had been so desperate to flee that she had taken the first offer on the place. He had intended to do the same, to assess the state of disrepair and put in the lowest possible offer, at least to start with.

'That's right—and if you don't have an animal, and don't need my services, then why the heck are you here?'

'This is ridiculous. It's freezing out here. I refuse to have a conversation in sub-zero temperatures.'

'I'm afraid I don't feel comfortable letting you into my house.' Becky squinted up at him. She was a mere five-foot-four and he absolutely towered over her. He was a tall, powerfully built stranger who had arrived in a frivolous boy-racer car out of the blue and she was on her own out here. No one would hear her scream for help. Should she *need* help.

Theo was outraged. No one, but no one, had ever had the temerity to say anything like that to him in his life before, least of all a woman. 'Exactly *what* are you suggesting?' he asked with withering cool, and Becky reddened but stoutly stood her ground.

'I don't know you.' She tilted her chin at a mutinous angle, challenging him to disagree with her. Every pore and fibre of her being was alert to him. It was as though, for the first time in her life, she was *aware* of her body, *aware* of her femininity, aware of her breasts—heavy and pushing against her bra—aware of her stiff and sensitive nipples, aware of her nakedness beneath her thick layer of clothes. Her discomfort was intense and bewildering.

'You could be *anyone*. I thought you were here because you needed my help with an animal, but you don't, so who the heck are you and why do you think I would let you into *my* house?'

'*Your* house?' Cool grey eyes skirted the rambling building and its surrounding fields. 'You're a little young to be the proud owner of a house this size, aren't you?'

'I'm older than you think.' Becky rushed into self-defence mode. 'And, not that it's any of your business, but yes, this house is mine. Or at least, I'm in charge while my parents are abroad and, that being the case, I won't be letting you inside. I don't even know your name.'

'Theo Rushing.' Some of the jigsaw immediately fell into place. He had expected to descend on the owners of the property. He hadn't known what, precisely, he would find but he had not been predisposed to be charitable to anyone who could have taken advantage of a distraught young woman, as his mother had been at the time.

At any rate, he had come with his cheque book, but without the actual owners at hand his cheque book was as useful as a three-pound note, because the belligerent little ball in front of him would not be able to make any decisions about anything.

Furthermore, she struck him as just the sort who *would* bite off the hand clutching the bank notes, or at least try and persuade her parents to...

He was accustomed to women wanting to please him. Faced with narrowed, suspicious eyes and the body language of a guard dog about to attack, he was forced to concede that announcing the purpose for his visit might not be such a good idea.

'I'm here to buy this cottage so you'll find yourself without a roof over your head in roughly a month and a half' wasn't going to win him brownie points.

He wanted the cottage and he was going to get it but he would have to be a little creative in how he handled the situation now.

He felt an unusual rush of adrenaline.

Theo had attained such meteoric heights over the years that the thrill of the challenge had been lost. When you could have anything you wanted, you increasingly lost interest in the things that should excite. Nothing was exciting if you didn't have to work to get it and that, he thought suddenly, included women.

Getting this cottage would be a challenge and he liked the thought of that.

'And I'm here...' He looked around him at the thick black sky. He had planned to arrive early afternoon but the extraordinary delays had dumped him here as darkness was beginning to fall. It had fallen completely now and there were no street lights to alleviate the unlit sky or to illuminate the fast falling snow.

His eyes returned to the woman in front of him. She was so heavily bundled up that he reckoned they could spend the next five hours out here and she would be immune to the freezing cold. He, on the other hand, having not expected to leave London and end up in a tundra, could not have been less well-prepared for the silent but deadly onslaught of the weather. Cashmere coats were all well and good in London but out here…

Waiting for an answer before she dispatched him without further ado, Becky could not help but stare. He was so beautiful that it almost hurt to tear her eyes away. In those crazy, faraway days, when she had been consumed by Freddy, she had enjoyed looking at him, had liked his regular, kind features, the gentleness of his expression and the warmth of his brown, puppy-dog eyes.

But she had never felt like this. There was something fascinating, *mesmerising*, about the play of shadow and darkness on his angular, powerful face. He was the last word in everything that *wasn't* gentle or kind and yet the pull she felt was overwhelming.

'Yes?' She clenched her gloved fists in the capacious pockets of her waterproof, knee-length, fleece-lined anorak. 'You're here because…?'

'Lost.' Theo spread his arm wide to encompass the lonely wilderness around him. 'Lost, and you're right—in a car that's not very clever when it comes to ice and snow. I'm not…accustomed to country roads and my satnav has had a field day trying to navigate its way to where I was planning on ending up.'

Lost. It made sense. Once you left the main roads behind—and that was remarkably easy to do—you could easily find yourself in a honeycomb of winding, unlit country lanes that would puzzle the best cartographer.

But that didn't change the fact that she was out here on her own in this house and he was still a stranger.

He read her mind. 'Look, I understand that you might feel vulnerable out here if you're on your own...' And she was, because there was no rush to jump in and warn him of an avenging boyfriend or husband wending his weary way back. 'But you will be perfectly safe if you let me in. The only reason I'm asking to be let in at all is because the weather's getting worse, and if I get into that car and try and make my way back to the bright lights I have no idea where I'll end up.'

Becky glanced at the racy, impractical sports car turning white as the snow gathered on it. *In a ditch*, was written all over its impractical bonnet.

Would her conscience allow her to send him off into the night, knowing that he would probably end up having an accident? What if the skittish car skidded off the road into one of the many trees and there was a fatality?

What if he ended up trapped in wreckage somewhere on an isolated country lane? If nothing else, he would perish from hypothermia, because his choice of clothing was as impractical for the weather as his choice of car.

'One night,' she said. 'And then I get someone to come and fetch you, first thing in the morning. I don't care if you have to leave the car here or not.'

'One night,' Theo murmured in agreement.

Becky felt the race of something dangerous slither through her.

She would give him shelter for one night and one night only...

What harm could come from that?

CHAPTER TWO

THE HOUSE SEEMED to shrink in size the minute he walked in. He'd fetched his computer from his car but that was all and Becky looked at him with a frown.

'Is that all you brought with you?'

'You still haven't told me your name.' The house was clearly on its last legs. Theo was no surveyor but that much was obvious. He now looked directly at her as he slowly removed his coat.

'Rebecca. Becky.' She watched as he carelessly slung his coat over one of the hooks by the front door. She could really appreciate his lean muscularity, now he was down to the jumper and trousers, and her mouth went dry.

This was as far out of her comfort zone as it was possible to get. Ever since Freddy, she had retreated into herself, content to go out as part of a group, to mingle with old friends—some of whom, like her, had returned to the beautiful Cotswolds, but to raise families. She hadn't actively chosen to discourage men but, as it happened, they had been few and far between. Twice she had been asked out on dates and twice she had decided that friendship was more valuable than the possibility of romance.

Truthfully, when she tried to think about relationships, she drew a blank. She wanted someone thoughtful and caring and those sorts of guys were already snapped up.

The guys who had asked her out had known her since for ever, and she knew for a fact that one of them was still recovering from a broken heart and had only asked her out on the rebound.

The other, the son of one of the farmers whom she had visited on call-out on several occasions, was nice enough, but nice enough just wasn't sufficient.

Or maybe she was being too fussy. That thought had occurred to her. When you were on your own for long enough, you grew careful, wary of letting anyone into your world, protective of your space. Was that what was happening to her?

At any rate, her comfort zone was on the verge of disappearing permanently unless she chose to stay where she was and travel long distances to another job.

She decided that inviting Theo in was good practice for what lay in store for her. She had opened her door to a complete stranger and she knew, with some weird gut instinct, that he was no physical threat to her.

In fact, seeing him in the unforgiving light in the hall did nothing to lessen the impact of his intense, sexual vitality. It was laughable to think that he would have any interest in her as anything other than someone offering refuge from the gathering snow storm.

'I can show you to one of the spare rooms.' Becky flushed because she could feel herself staring again. 'I don't keep them heated, but I'll turn the radiator on, and it shouldn't take too long to warm up. You might want to…freshen up.'

'I would love nothing more,' Theo drawled. 'Unfortunately, no change of clothing. Would you happen to have anything I could borrow? Husband's old gardening clothes? Boyfriend's…?' He wondered whether she intended to spend the rest of the evening in the shapeless anorak and mud-stained boots. She had to be the least fashion-conscious woman he had ever met in his entire life, yet for the life of him he was still captivated by something about her.

The eyes, the unruly hair still stuffed under the woolly hat, the lack of war paint…what was it?

He had no idea but he hadn't felt this alive in a woman's presence for a while.

Then again, it had been a while since he had been in the presence of any woman who wasn't desperate to attract his attention. There was a lot to be said for novelty.

'I can let you borrow something.' Becky shifted from foot to foot. She was boiling in the coat but somehow she didn't like the thought of stripping down to her jeans and top in front of him. Those sharp, lazy eyes of his made her feel all hot and bothered. 'My dad left some of his stuff in the wardrobe in the room you'll be in. You can have a look and see what might be able to work for you. And if you leave your stuff outside the bedroom door, then I guess I can stick it in the washing machine.'

'You needn't do that.'

'You're soaked,' Becky said flatly. 'Your clothes will smell if you leave them to dry without washing them first.'

'In that case, I won't refuse your charming offer,' Theo said drily and Becky flushed.

Very conscious of his eyes on her, she preceded him up the stairs, pointedly ignoring the bucket gathering water on the ground from the leaking roof, and flung open the door to one of the spare bedrooms. Had she actually thought things through when she had fled back to the family home, she would have realised that the 'cottage' was a cottage in name only. In reality, it was reasonably large, with five bedrooms and outbuildings in the acres outside. It was far too big for her and she wondered, suddenly, whether her parents had felt sorry for her and offered to allow her to stay there through pity. They hadn't known about Freddy and her broken heart but what must they have felt when she had dug her heels in and insisted on returning to the family home while Alice, already far flown from the nest, was busily making marriage plans so that the next phase of her life could begin?

Becky cringed.

Her parents would never, ever have denied her the cottage but they weren't rich. They had bought somewhere tiny in France when her grandmother had died, and they had both continued working part-time, teaching in the local school.

Becky had always thought it a brilliant way of integrating into life in the French town, but what if they'd only done that because they needed the money?

While she stayed here, paying a peppercorn rent and watching the place gradually fall apart at the seams…

She was struck by her own selfishness and it was something that had never occurred to her until now.

She would phone, she decided. Feel out the ground. After all, whether she liked it or not, her lifestyle was going to change dramatically once she was out of a job.

Theo looked at her and wondered what was going through her mind. He hadn't failed to notice the way she had neatly stepped past a bucket in the corridor which was quarter-full from the leaking roof.

It was startling enough that a woman of her age would choose to live out in the sticks, however rewarding her job might be, but it was even more startling that, having chosen to live out in the sticks, she continued to live in a house that was clearly on the verge of giving up the fight.

When he bought this cottage, he would be doing her a favour by forcing her out into the real world.

Where life happened.

Rather than her staying here…hiding away…which surely was what she was doing…?

Hiding from what? he wondered. He was a little amused at how involved he temporarily was in mentally providing an answer to that ridiculous question.

But if he had to get her onside, manoeuvre her into a position where she might see the sense of not standing in his way when it came to buying the cottage, then wouldn't it help to get to know her a little?

Of course, there was no absolute necessity to get anyone onside. He could simply bypass her and head directly to the parents. Make them an offer they couldn't refuse. But for once he wasn't quite ruthless enough to go down that road. There was something strangely alluring underneath the guard-dog belligerence. And he was not forgetting that there were times when money *didn't* open the door you wanted opening. If he bypassed her and leant on the parents, there was a real risk of them uniting with their daughter to shut him out permanently, whatever sums of money he chose to throw at them. Family loyalty could be a powerful wild card, and he should know… Wasn't family loyalty the very thing that had brought him to this semi-derelict cottage?

She was switching on the ancient heating, opening the wardrobe so that she could show him where the clothes were kept, fetching a towel from the corridor, dumping it on the bed and then informing him that the bathroom was just down the corridor, but that he would have to make sure that the toilet wasn't flushed before he turned on the shower or else he might end up with third-degree burns.

Theo walked slowly towards her and then stopped a few inches away.

When Becky breathed, she could breathe him in, masculinity mixed with the cold winter air, a heady, heady mix. Leaning against the doorframe, she blinked, suddenly unsteady on her feet.

He had amazing lashes, long, dark and thick. She wanted to ask him where he was from, because there was an exotic strain running through him that was quite… captivating.

He had shoved up the sleeves of his jumper and, even though she wasn't actually looking, she was very much aware of his forearms, the fine, dark hair on them, the flex of muscle and sinew…

Her breathing was so sluggish that it crossed her mind… *was it actually physically possible to forget how to breathe*?

'I don't get why you live here.' Theo was genuinely curious.

'Wh-what do you mean?' Becky stammered.

'The house needs a lot of work doing to it. I could understand if your parents wanted you in situ while work was being done but…can I call you Becky?…there's a bucket out in the corridor. And how long do you intend emptying it before you face the unpalatable fact that the roof probably needs replacing?'

Hard on the heels of the uncomfortable thoughts that had been preying on her mind, Theo's remarks struck home with deadly accuracy.

'I don't see that the state of this house is any of your business!' Bright patches of colour stained her cheeks. 'You're here for a night, *one night*, and only because I wouldn't have been able to live with myself if I had sent you on your way in this weather. But that doesn't give you the right to…to…'

'Talk?'

'You're not *talking*, you're—'

'I'm probably saying things that have previously occurred to you, things you may have chosen to ignore.' He
shrugged, unwillingly intrigued by the way she was so
patently uninterested in trying to impress him. 'If you'd
rather I didn't, then that's fine. I have some work to do
when I get downstairs and then we can pretend to have
an invigorating conversation about the weather.'

'I'll be downstairs.' This for want of anything more
coherent to say when she was so...*angry*...that he had
had the nerve to shoot his mouth off! He was rude beyond words!

But he wasn't wrong.

And this impertinent stranger had provided the impetus she needed to make that call to her parents. As soon
as she was in the kitchen, with the door firmly shut, because the man was as stealthy as a panther and obviously
didn't wait for invitations to speak his mind. There was
some beating around the bush but, yes, it *would* be rather
lovely if the house *was* sold, not that they would ever
dream of asking her to leave.

But...but...but...but.

Lots of *buts*, so that by the time Becky hung up fifteen minutes later she was in no doubt that not only was
she heading for unemployment but the leaking roof over
her head would not be hers for longer than it took for the
local estate agent to come along and offer a valuation.

Mind still whirring busily away, she headed back up
the stairs. She wished she could think more clearly and
see a way forward but the path ahead was murky. What if
she couldn't get a job? It should be easy but, then again,
she was in a highly specialised field. What if she did
manage to find a posting but it was in an even more re-

mote spot than this? Did she really want the years ahead to be spent in a practice in the wilds of Scotland? But weren't the more desirable posts in London, Manchester or Birmingham going to be the first to be filled?

And underneath all those questions was the dissatisfaction that had swamped her after she had spoken to her sister.

Her life had been put into harsh perspective. The time she had spent here now seemed to have been wasted. Instead of moving forward, she had stayed in the same place, pedalling furiously and getting nowhere.

She surfaced from her disquieting thoughts to find that, annoyingly, the clothes she had asked to be placed outside the bedroom door were not there.

Did the man think that he was staying in a hotel?

Did he imagine that it was okay for her to hang around like a chambermaid until he decided that he could be bothered to hand over his dirty laundry for her to do? She didn't even have to wash his clothes! She could have sent him on his way in musty, semi-damp trousers and a jumper that smelled of pond water.

He obviously thought that he was so important that he could do as he pleased. Speak to her as he pleased. Accept her hospitality whilst antagonising her because he found it entertaining.

She had no idea how important or unimportant he was but, quite aside from the snazzy little racing-red number and the designer clothing, there was something about him that screamed *wealth*.

Or maybe it was *power*.

Well, none of that impressed *her*. She'd never had time for anyone who thought that money was the be all and end all. It just wasn't the way she had been brought up.

It was what was inside that counted. It was why, although Freddy had not been the one for her, there was a guy out there who was, a guy who had the sterling qualities of kindness, quiet intelligence and self-deprecating humour.

And, having ducked the dating scene for years, she would get back out there...because if she didn't then this was the person she would be in the years to come, entrenched in her singledom, godmother to all and sundry and maid of honour to her friends as they tied the knot and moved on with their fulfilling lives.

Swamped by sudden self-pity, she absently shoved open the door to the spare room, which was ajar, and... stopped. Her legs stopped moving, her hand froze on the door knob and her brain went into instant shutdown.

She didn't know where to look and somewhere inside she knew that it didn't matter because wherever she looked she would still end up seeing him. Tall, broadshouldered, his body an amazing burnished bronze. She would still see the hardness of his six pack and the length of his muscular legs, the legs of an athlete.

Aside from a pair of low-slung boxers, he was completely naked.

Becky cleared her throat and opened her mouth and nothing emerged but an inarticulate noise.

'I was just about to stick the clothes outside...'

Without the woollen hat pulled down over her head, her hair was long, tumbling down her back in a cascade of unruly, dark curls, and without the layers upon layers of shriekingly unfashionable arctic gear...

She wasn't the round little beach ball he had imagined. Even with the loose-fitting striped rugby shirt, he could see that she had the perfect hourglass figure. News obviously hadn't reached this part of the world that the fashionable trend these days leaned towards long, thin and toned to athletic perfection, even if the exercise involved to get there never saw the outside of an expensive gym.

He could feel his whole body reacting to the sight of her lush curves and he hurriedly turned away, because a pair of boxers was no protection against an erection.

He was staring. Becky stood stock-still, conscious of herself and her body in ways she had never been before. Why was he staring at her like that? Was he even aware that he was doing it?

She couldn't believe that he was staring at her because she was the most glamorous woman he had ever set eyes on. She wasn't born yesterday and she knew that when it came to looks, well, a career could not be made out of hers. Alice had got the looks and she, Becky, had got the brains and it had always seemed like a fair enough deal to her.

He'd turned away now, thankfully putting on some ancient track pants her father had left behind and an even more ancient jumper, and by the time he turned back around to face her she wondered whether she had imagined those cool, grey eyes on her, skirting over her body.

Yes, she thought a little shakily. Of course she had. *She* had stared at *him* because he looked like a Greek god. *She* on the other hand was as average as they came.

Should she feel threatened? She was alone in this house…

She didn't feel threatened. She felt…excited. Something wicked and daring stirred inside her and she promptly knocked it back.

'The clothes.' She found her voice, one hand outstretched, watching as he gathered items of clothing and strolled towards her. 'I'll make sure they're washed and ready for you tomorrow morning.'

'First thing…before I'm sent on my way,' Theo murmured, still startled at the fierce grip of his libido that had struck from nowhere.

She couldn't wait to escape, he thought with a certain amount of disbelief.

Something had passed between them just then. Had she even been aware of it? A charge of electricity had shaken him and she hadn't been unaffected. He'd seen the reaction in the widening of her eyes as she had looked at him, and the stillness of her body language, as though one false move might have led her to do something…rash.

Did *rash* happen out here? he wondered. Or was she out here because she was escaping from something rash? Was the awkward, blushing, argumentative vet plagued by guilt over a misspent past? Had she thrown herself into a one-way relationship to nowhere with a con man? A married man? A rampant womaniser who had used her and tossed her aside? The possibilities were endless.

She certainly wasn't out here for the money. That bucket on the landing said it all. She might be living rent free at the place but she certainly wasn't earning enough to keep it maintained. Old houses consumed money with the greed of a gold-digger on the make.

'What if it's still snowing in the morning?'

She was clutching the bundle of clothes like a talisman and staring up at him with those amazing bright blue eyes. Her lips were parted. When she circled a nervous tongue over them, Theo had to fight down an urge to reach out and pull her against him.

'It won't be.'

'If you weren't prepared to risk my life by sending me on my way, then will you be prepared to risk someone else's life by asking them to come and collect me and take me away?'

'I could drive you myself. I have a four-wheel drive. It's okay in conditions like this.'

'When I knocked on your door...' Theo leant against the door frame '...I never expected someone like you to open it'

'What do you mean *someone like me*?' Becky stiffened, primed for some kind of thinly veiled insult.

Theo didn't say anything for a couple of seconds. Instead, he watched her, head tilted to one side, until she looked away, blushing. Very gently, he tilted her face back to his.

'You're on the defensive. Why?'

'Why do you think? I...I don't know you.' The feel of his cool finger resting lightly on her chin was as scorching-hot as the imprint from a branding iron.

'What do you think I'm going to do? When I said *someone like you*, I meant someone young. I expected someone much older to be living this far out in the countryside.'

'I told you, the house belongs to my parents. I'm just here... Look, I'm going to head downstairs, wash these things...' Her feet and brain were not communicating because, instead of spinning around and backing out of the room, she remained where she was, glued to the spot.

She wanted him to remove his hand...she wanted him to do more with it, wanted him to curve it over her face and then slide it across her shoulders, wanted him to find the bare flesh of her stomach and then the swell of her breasts... She didn't want to hear anything he had to say, yet he was making her think, and how could that be a bad thing?

She barely recognised her voice and she certainly didn't know what was going on with her body.

'Okay.' He stepped back, hand dropping to his side.

For a few seconds, Becky hovered, then she cleared her throat and stepped out of the room backwards.

By the time he joined her in the kitchen, the clothes were in the washing machine and she had regained her composure.

Theo looked at her for a few seconds from the doorway. She had her back to him and was busy chopping vegetables, while as background noise the television was giving an in-depth report of the various areas besieged by snow when spring should have sprung. He felt that her house would shortly be featured because there was no sign of the snow letting up.

Before he had come down, he had done his homework, nosed into a few of the rooms and seen for himself what he had suspected from the bucket on the landing catching water from the leaking roof.

The house was on its last legs. Did he think that he was doing anything underhand in checking out the property before he made an offer? No. He'd come here to conduct a business deal and, if things had been slightly thrown off course, nothing had fundamentally changed. The key thing remained the business deal.

And was the woman peeling the vegetables an unexpected part of acquiring what he wanted? Was she now part of the business deal that had to be secured?

In a way, yes.

And he was not in the slightest ashamed of taking this pragmatic view. Why should he be? This was the man he was and it was how he had succeeded beyond even his own wildest expectations.

If you allowed your emotions to guide you, you ended up a victim of whatever circumstances came along to blow you off course.

He had no intention of ever being one of life's victims.

His mother had so much to give, but she had allowed her damaged heart to take control of her entire future, so that, in the end, whatever she'd had to give to anyone else had dried up. Wasn't that one reason why she was so consumed with the thought of having grandchildren? Of seeing him married off?

Because her ability to give had to go somewhere and he was the only recipient.

That was what emotions did to a person. They stripped you of your ability to think. That was why he had never done commitment and never would. Commitment led to relationships and relationships were almost always train wrecks waiting to happen. Lawyers were kept permanently busy sorting out those train wrecks and making lots of money in the process.

He had his life utterly in control and that was the way he liked it.

He had no doubt that whatever had brought Becky to this place was a story that might tug on someone else's heartstrings. *His* heartstrings would be blessedly immune to any tugging. He would be able to find out about her and persuade her to accept that this was no place for her to be. When, inevitably, the house was sold from under her feet, she would not try and put up a fight, wouldn't try and coax her parents into letting her stay on.

He would have long disappeared from her life. He would have been nothing more than a stranger who had landed for a night and then moved on. But she would remember what he had said and she would end up thanking him.

Because, frankly, this was no place for her to be. It wasn't healthy. She was far too young.

He looked at the rounded swell of her derrière...

Far too young and far too sexy.

'What are you cooking?'

Becky swung round to see him lounging against the door frame. Her father was a little shorter and reedier than Theo. Theo looked as though he had been squashed into clothes a couple of sizes too small. And he was barefoot. Her eyes shot back to his face to find that he was staring right back at her with a little smile.

'Pasta. Nothing special. And you can help.' She turned her back on him and felt him close the distance between them until he was standing next to her, at which point she pointed to some onions and slid a small, sharp knife towards him. 'You've asked me a lot of questions,' she said, eyes sliding across to his hands and then hurriedly sliding back to focus on what she was doing. 'But I don't know anything about you.'

'Ask away.'

'Where do you live?'

'London.' Theo couldn't remember the last time he'd chopped an onion. Were they always this fiddly?

'And what were you doing in this part of the world? Aside from getting lost?'

Theo felt a passing twinge of guilt. 'Taking my car for some exercise,' he said smoothly. 'And visiting one or two…familiar spots en route.'

'Seems an odd thing to do at this time of year,' Becky mused. 'On your own.'

'Does it?' Theo dumped the half-peeled onion. 'Is there anything to drink in this house or do vets not indulge just in case they get a midnight call and need to be in their car within minutes, tackling the dangerous country lanes in search of a sick animal somewhere?'

Becky stopped what she was doing and looked at him, and at the poor job he had made of peeling an onion.

'I'm not really into domestic chores.' Theo shrugged.

'There's wine in the fridge. I'm not on call this evening and, as it happens, I don't get hundreds of emergency calls at night. I'm not a doctor. Most of my patients can wait a few hours and, if they can't, everyone around here knows where the nearest animal hospital is. And you haven't answered my question. Isn't it a bit strange for you to be here on your own...just driving around?'

Theo took his time pouring the wine, then he handed her a glass and settled into a chair at the kitchen table.

His own penthouse was vast and ultra-modern. He didn't care for cosy, although he had to admit that there was something to be said for it in the middle of a blizzard with the snow turning everything white outside. This was a cosy kitchen. Big cream Aga...worn pine table with mismatched chairs...flagstone floor that had obviously had underfloor heating installed at some point, possibly before the house had begun buckling under the effect of old age, because it wasn't bloody freezing underfoot...

'Just driving around,' he said slowly, truthfully, 'is a luxury I can rarely afford.' He thought about his life—high-voltage, adrenaline-charged, pressurised, the life of someone who made millions. There was no time for standing still. 'I seldom stop, and even when I do, I am permanently on call.' He smiled crookedly, at odds with himself for giving in to the unheard of temptation to confide.

'What on earth do you do?' Becky leant against the counter and stared at him with interest.

'I...buy things, do them up and sell them on. Some of them I keep for myself because I'm greedy.'

'What sorts of things?'

'Companies.'

Becky stared at him thoughtfully. The sauce was simmering nicely on the Aga. She went to sit opposite him, nursing her glass of wine.

Looking at her, Theo wondered if she had any idea of just how wealthy he was. She would now be getting the picture that he wasn't your average two-up, two-down, one holiday a year, nine-to-five kind of guy and he wondered whether, like every other single woman he had ever met, she was doing the maths and working out how profitable it might be to get to know him better.

'Poor you,' Becky said at last and he frowned.

'Come again?'

'It must be awful never having time to yourself. I don't have much but what I do have I really appreciate. I'd hate it if I had to get in my car and drive out into the middle of nowhere just to have some uninterrupted peace.'

She laughed, relaxed for the first time since he had landed on her doorstep. 'Our parents always made a big thing about money not being the most important thing in life.' Her bright turquoise eyes glinted with sudden humour. 'Alice and I used to roll our eyes but they were right. That's why...' she looked around her at the kitchen, where, as a family, they had spent countless hours together '...I can appreciate all this quiet, which I know you don't understand.'

The prospect of saying goodbye to the family house made her eyes mist over. 'There's something wonderfully peaceful about being here. I don't need the crowds of a city. I never have or I never would have returned here after... Well, this is where I belong.' And the thought of finding somewhere else to call home felt like such a huge mountain to climb that she blinked back a bout of severe self-pity. Her parents had moved on as had Alice. So could she.

Theo, watching her, felt a stab of alarm. A pep talk

wasn't going to get her packing her belongings and moving on and a wad of cash, by all accounts, wasn't going to cut it with her parents.

When was the last time he had met someone who wasn't impressed by money and what it could buy?

His mother, of course, who had never subscribed to his single-minded approach to making money, even though, as he had explained on countless occasions, making money per se was a technicality. The only point to having money was the security it afforded and that was worth its weight in gold. Surely, he had argued, she could see that—especially considering her life had been one of making ends meet whilst trying to bring up a child on her own?

He moved in circles where money talked, where people were impressed by it. The women he met enjoyed what he could give them. His was the sort of vast, bottomless wealth that opened doors, that conferred absolute freedom.

And what, he wondered, was wrong with that?

'Touching,' he said coolly. 'Clearly none of your family members are in agreement, considering they're nowhere to be seen. The opposite, in fact. They've done a runner and cleared off to a different country.'

'Do you know what?' Becky said with heartfelt sincerity. 'You may think you're qualified to look down your nose at other people who don't share your…your… materialism, but I feel sorry for anyone who thinks it's worth spending every minute of every day working! I feel sorry for someone who never has time off to just *do nothing.* Do you ever relax? Put your feet up? Listen to music? Or just watch television?' Becky's voice rang with self-righteous sincerity but she was guiltily aware that she was far from being the perfectly content person she was making herself out to be.

She hadn't rushed back to the cottage because she couldn't be without the vast, open peaceful spaces a second longer. She'd rushed back because her heart had been broken. And she hadn't stayed here because she'd been seduced by all the wonderful, tranquil downtime during which she listened to music or watched television with her feet up. She'd stayed because she'd fallen into a job and had then been too apathetic to do anything else about moving on with her life in a more dynamic way.

And it wasn't fun listening out for leaks. It wasn't fun waiting for the heating to pack up. And it certainly wasn't fun to know that, in another country, the rest of her family was busy feeling sorry for her and waiting for her to up sticks so that the house could be sold and valuable capital released.

'I relax,' Theo said softly.

'Huh?' She focused on a sharply indrawn breath, blinking like a rabbit caught in the headlights at the lazy, sexy smile curving his mouth.

'In between the work, I actually do manage to take time off to relax. It's just that my form of relaxation doesn't happen to include watching television or listening to music… But I can assure you that it's every bit as satisfying, if somewhat more energetic…'

CHAPTER THREE

'WHAT DO *YOU* do here?'

'What do you mean?' Becky asked in sudden confusion.

'To relax.' Theo sprawled back, angling the chair so that he could loosely cross his legs, ankle resting on thigh, one arm slung over the back of the chair, the other toying with the wine glass, twirling it slowly between his long fingers as he continued to look at her.

'I mean,' he continued pensively, 'it's all well and good killing time in front of the television with your feet up, while you congratulate yourself on how peaceful it is, but what else do you get up to when you've had your fill of the great open spaces and the lack of noise?'

'I grew up here' was all Becky could find to say.

'University must have been a very different change of scenery for you,' Theo mused. 'Which university did you go to?'

He could see her reluctance to divulge any personal details. It made him want to pry harder, to extract as much information as he could from her. Her dewy skin was pink and flushed. In a minute, she would briskly stand up and dodge his personal attack on her by busying herself in front of the Aga.

'Cambridge.'

'Impressive. And then you decided, after going to one of the top universities on the planet, that you would return here so that you could get a job at a small practice in the middle of nowhere?'

'Like I said, you wouldn't understand.'

'You're right. I don't. And you still haven't told me what you do for relaxation around here.'

'I barely have time to relax.' Becky stood up abruptly, uncomfortable with his questioning. She rarely found her motives questioned.

'But I thought you said...' A smile quirked at the corner of Theo's mouth.

'Yes, well,' snapped Becky, turning her back to him, more than a little flustered.

'But when you do...?' Theo followed her to where she was standing, clearing an already tidy counter.

He gently relieved her of the cloth and looked down at her.

Becky had no idea what was happening. Was this flirting? She had successfully convinced herself that there was no way the man could have any interest in her, aside from polite interest towards someone who had agreed to let him stay for the night because of the poor weather conditions. But when he looked at her the way he was looking at her now...

Her mind broke its leash and raced off in all sorts of crazy directions.

He was obnoxious. Of course he was, with his generalisations, his patronising assertions and that typical rich man's belief that money was the only thing that mattered.

He was just the sort of guy she had no time for.

But he was so outrageously beautiful and that was what gripped her imagination and held it. That was what was making her body react with such treacherous heat to his smoky grey eyes.

He'd painted a picture for her when he'd told her how he relaxed. *He hadn't had to go into details because in a few sentences she had pictured him naked...aroused... focusing all that glorious, masculine attention on one woman...*

'You surely must get a little lonely out here?' Theo murmured softly. 'However much you love the peace and isolation.'

'I...'

Her eyelids fluttered and her lips parted on an automatic denial of any such thing.

Theo drew in a sharp breath, riveted by the sight of those full, plump lips. She had no idea how alluring that mixture of apprehension and innocence was. It made him want to touch, even though he knew that it would be a mistake. This wasn't one of those women who'd stopped being green round the ears when they were sixteen. Whatever experiences this woman had had, whatever had driven her back to this house—and he was certain that something had—she was innocent.

He stepped back and raked his fingers through his hair, breaking the electric connection between them.

Becky was trembling. She could feel the tremor running through her body, as though she had had a shock and was still feeling the aftermath of it, even though he had returned to the table to sit back down. She couldn't look at him as he picked up the conversation, making sure to steer clear of anything personal.

He asked her about the sort of situations she had to deal with out in the country... How many were in the practice? Had she always wanted to be a vet? Why had she chosen that over a conventional medicine course?

He didn't ask her again whether she was lonely.

He didn't ask her why she had chosen to retreat to the country to live when she could have had a job anywhere in the country.

When he looked at her, it was without that lazy, assessing speculation that made her blood thicken and made her break out in a cold sweat.

He complimented her on the meal and asked her about her diet, about how she managed to fit in her meals with the hours she worked.

He could not have been more meticulously polite if he had been obeying orders with a gun held to his head and she hated it.

His arrival at the house was the most exciting thing that had happened to her in a long time and it had occurred just when she had been questioning her whole life, putting it into perspective, trying to figure out a way forward. It had occurred hard on the heels of her sister's phone call, which had stirred up a grey, sludgy mix of emotion in her, some of which she didn't like.

It also felt as though fate had sent him along to challenge her.

And how was she going to respond to that challenge? By running away? By retreating? She was going to be challenged a lot more when her job came to an end and the roof over her head was sold, and what was she going to do then? Dive for cover, close her eyes and hope for the best?

Where was the harm in getting into some practice now when it came to dealing with the unexpected? It wasn't as though there would be any repercussions, was it? You could bare your soul to a stranger on a plane and then walk away when the plane landed, safe in the knowledge that you wouldn't clap eyes on that person again, so if they happened to be a receptacle for all your secrets, what difference would that make?

She felt as though she had been on standby for someone just like him to come along and shake her world up a little because things had settled in a way that frightened her.

'It does get lonely,' she said, putting down her fork and spoon and cupping her chin in the palm of her hand to look at him. She cleared her throat, realising that this was something she had never said aloud to anyone. 'I mean, I'm busy most of the time, and of course I have friends here. It's a small place. Everyone knows everyone else and, since I returned, I've caught up with friends who went to school with me. It's nice enough but...' She took a deep breath. 'You're right. Sometimes, it gets a little lonely...'

Theo sat back to look at her narrowly. He had angled to find out more about her. He had reasoned that knowledge was power. To find out about her would help him when it came to buying the house. But, more than that, he had been strangely curious, curious to find out what had brought her and kept her here.

Now she was telling him—was it a good idea to encourage her in her confidences?

She wasn't the confiding sort. He could see that in the soft, embarrassed flush in her cheeks, as though she was doing something against her better judgement.

'Why are you telling me this?' he asked softly and Becky looked at him from under her lashes.

'Why not?'

'Because you've been resisting my questions ever since I turned up here and started asking them.'

Becky's flush deepened.

'I don't know you,' she said honestly, shrugging. 'And

once you leave my house I'll never see you again. You're not my type—you're not the sort of person I would ever want to continue having any sort of friendship with, despite the weird way we've happened to meet.'

'Such irresistible charm...' he murmured, catching her eye and countering her sheepishness with raised eyebrows.

Becky laughed and then warmed when he smiled back, a watchful, assessing smile. 'A girl doesn't get much chance to be irresistibly charming out here in the sticks,' she said. 'The livestock don't appreciate it.'

'But there's more than livestock out here, isn't there?' Theo prodded.

'Not much,' Becky confessed. She grimaced and then looked away, down to the wine glass which appeared to be empty. He had brought the bottle to the table and now he reached across to top her up. 'I say that I'm not on call-out twenty-four seven,' she laughed. 'Let's hope I don't get an emergency call tonight because I might just end up with my car in a ditch.'

'Surely no one would expect you to go out in weather like this?' Theo looked at her, startled, and she laughed again.

She had a lovely laugh, soft, ever so slightly self-conscious, the sort of laugh that automatically made you want to smile.

'No. Although I *have* had emergencies in snow before where I've had no choice but to get into my car, head out and hope for the best. Sheep. They sometimes have poor timing when it comes to lambing. They don't usually care whether it's snowing or whether it's three in the morning.'

'So just the demanding sheep to get your attention...' He considered that, in the absence of a significant other, she would be as free as a bird should she find herself having to leave the house at short notice.

To somewhere—he mentally justified the inevitable—where there might be more for a girl of her age than sheep and livestock.

'I don't suppose someone like you ever feels…like you're not too sure where you're going or what the next step might be.'

The question caught him by surprise because it wasn't often anyone ignored his 'no trespass' signs to ask anything as outrageously personal, and for a few seconds he contemplated not answering. But, then again, why not? Like she had so aptly said, they were ships passing in the night.

And besides, he liked that shy, tentative look on her face. It was so different from the feisty little minx who had first greeted him at the front door. He liked the fact that she was opening up to him. Normally uninterested in most women's predictable back stories—which were always spun as a prelude to someone trying to get to him—he had to admit that he was keen to hear hers.

She wanted nothing from him and that was liberating. He thought that it allowed him actually to *be himself*.

Of course, within certain limits, considering he had chosen to keep her in the dark about his real reasons for descending on her like a bolt from the blue, but there was no such thing as absolute truth between people, was there?

'No,' he drawled. 'I make it my business to always know where I'm going and I certainly have never been wrong-footed when it comes to the future.'

'Never?' Becky laughed uncertainly. He was so overwhelming, so blindingly self-assured. Those were character traits that should have left her cold but in him they were sexy, seductive, almost endearing. 'Nothing has ever happened in your life that you haven't been able to control?'

Theo frowned. Outside, through the kitchen window, he could see the driving fall of white, as fine and fierce as a dust storm, lit up and dazzling in the little patch outside the window where a light had been switched on.

Inside was warm and mellow. He hadn't felt so unstressed in a while and he recalled why he had been stressed for the past several months. Nothing to do with work. The stress of work was something he enjoyed, something he needed to survive, the way a plant needs rain or sun. He had been stressed out by his mother. This was the first time he could think about her without his gut tightening up.

'My mother has been ill,' he heard himself say abruptly. 'A stroke. Out of the blue. No one saw it coming, least of all me. So, yes, that could be categorised as something that has happened that has been out of my control.'

Becky wanted to reach across and squeeze his hand because he looked awkward with the confession. She wasn't accustomed to pouring her heart out to anyone and, clearly, neither was he. Not that she wouldn't have been able to see that for herself after five minutes in his company.

'I'm sorry. How is she now? How is your father dealing with it? And the rest of your family? Sometimes, it's almost harder for the family members.'

Theo wondered how he had managed to end up here, with a virtual stranger leaning towards him, face wreathed with sympathy.

'There's just me,' he said shortly. 'My father died…a long time ago and I'm an only child.'

'That's tough.' Becky thought of her own family arrangements.

'Do you feel sorry for me?' he prompted with silky smoothness. He smiled slowly, very slowly, and watched as the blood crept up to her hairline. She wanted to look away, but she couldn't, and that gave him a heady kick because the oldest game in the book was being played now and he liked that.

He liked it a lot more than spilling his guts like one of those emotional, touchy-feely types he had never had time for.

This was safe ground and known territory. When it came to sex, Theo was at home, and this was about sex. Why bother to beat about the bush? She wanted him and the feeling was mutual. He didn't understand why he found her so appealing, because she was not his type, but he did, and he wondered whether that had to do with the fact that for once there was no pressure. He wasn't even certain that she would take his hand if he offered it and allow herself to be led up to that bedroom of hers.

The uncertainty just lent another layer to the thrill of a chase he hadn't yet decided to embark upon.

Though she was so unknowingly sexy...

He wondered what she would look like without clothes on. He had to guess at a figure she was hell-bent on concealing and he was desperate to see what was there. He flexed his fingers and shifted.

'Of course I feel sorry for you,' Becky was saying with heartfelt sincerity. 'I'd be devastated if anything happened to one of my family.' She watched as he slowly eased his big body out of the chair. Her heart began to beat fast and it was beating even faster when he leaned over her to support himself on either side of her chair, caging her in.

She wanted to touch him. She wanted him to touch her. In no way did she feel in the slightest threatened by this tall, lean, powerful man physically dominating her with his presence.

She felt…feminine.

It was an unfamiliar feeling because femininity was something she had always presumed herself lacking. It went with good looks and both of those were the domain of her sister.

'How sorry?' Theo murmured huskily. Her excitement was contagious. He could feel it roaring through his veins, making him act in this unexpected way, because the caveman approach was just not his thing. He didn't sling women over his shoulder or rip their clothes off. That would have been on a par with beating his chest and swinging from tree to tree on a vine. But he wanted to sling this one over his shoulder, especially when she sat there, staring at him with those incredible eyes, chewing on her lower lip, refusing flippantly to give in to the massive charge of attraction between them.

'I…' Becky offered weakly. 'What's going on here?'

'Sorry?' Theo wondered whether he had misheard.

'I'm not sure I understand what's going on…'

'What do you think is going on? We're two adults and we're attracted to one another and what's going on is me making a pass at you…'

'Why?'

Theo straightened. He shot her a crooked smile and then perched on the edge of the table. 'This is a first for me.'

'What is?' Startled, Becky stared at him. She was so turned on that she could barely speak and she couldn't quite believe that this was happening. Not to her. Stuff like this never happened to her. She had always been the bookworm who attracted fellow bookworms. Face it, even Freddy had been a bookworm just like her. Guys like Theo didn't go for girls like her. They went for hot blondes in tight dresses who batted their eyelashes and knew what to do when it came to sex.

What did she know about sex? Nerves gripped her but the promise of that ride, with its speed, its thrills and its unbearable excitement, was much, much greater than any attack of nerves.

She wanted this.

'Never mind,' she said softly, eyes dipped. Her innate seriousness wanted to be reassured, wanted to be told that this was more than just sex, but of course it wasn't. It was purely about sex and that was part of its dragging appeal. This went against everything inside her and yet she couldn't resist its ferocious tug on all her senses.

'Look at me, Becky.'

She obeyed and waited with halted breath for him to say what he had to say.

'If you have any doubts at all, then say so right now and we both walk away from this.'

She shook her head and smiled, and Theo nodded. 'And Becky…' He leaned over her once again, his dark, lean face utterly serious. 'There's something I should tell you from the outset, just so that there are no misunderstandings. Don't invest in me and don't think that this is going to be the start of something big. It won't. I don't do relationships and, even if I did, we're from different worlds.'

He didn't do relationships and, even if he did, they were from different worlds…

He was giving her an out and he wasn't beating about the bush. This would be a one-night stand. She was going to hand her virginity over to someone who had made it clear that there was nothing between them bar physical attraction The one thing on which she had never placed any emphasis. Yet this was more than longing on her part. Her virginity felt like an albatross around her neck and she wanted to set herself free from it more than anything in the world.

'Message received and understood,' Becky murmured and blushed as he delivered her a slashing smile. 'You're not from my world either and, although I *do* do relationships, it would never, ever be with someone like you. So we're on the same page.' The dynamics of what happened next was making her perspire. Should she tell him that she was a virgin? No. Chances were he would never guess anyway...and she didn't want him to take fright and pull back.

'I've wanted you the minute I saw you,' Theo confessed unsteadily, fingers hooking under the waistband of the jogging bottoms he had borrowed.

'Even though I'm from a different world?' She tilted her chin up and stared at him.

'You've admitted the same about me' was his gruff response.

'I don't know why I find you attractive at all,' she muttered to herself and Theo laughed.

'Don't spare my ego, whatever you do.'

Their eyes tangled and she felt an affinity with him, this inappropriate stranger, that was so powerful it took her breath away. It was as if they were on exactly the same page, united, thinking as one, mixed up with one another as though they belonged.

Shaken, she stared at him.

Turned on beyond belief, Theo stayed her as she made to stand. 'Not yet,' he murmured. He stood in front of her and then he knelt and parted her legs, big hands on her inner thighs. Becky held her breath and then released it in a series of little gasps and sighs. She wanted to squirm. She wasn't naked but the way he was holding her, his position between her legs, made her feel exposed and daringly, recklessly wanton.

She flung back her head and half-closed her eyes. She felt his fingers dip under the waistband of her jeans and then the soft pop of the button being released, followed by the sound of the zipper being pulled down.

Everything was heightened.

She could hear the hammering of her heart against her rib cage, the raspy sound of her jerky breathing, the soft fluttering of her eyelids. She wriggled as he began to pull down her jeans.

This was surreal. The girl who had always thought that sex would be with someone she had given her heart to was desperate for a man who was just passing through. The girl who had quietly assumed that she'd *know* when love struck was being floored by something she had never anticipated—unbridled, hot, heady, sweat-inducing lust.

Cool air hit her legs. She half-opened her eyes and groaned softly, reaching out to curl her fingers in Theo's hair. He looked up and their eyes met.

'Enjoying yourself?' he asked in a wickedly soft voice and Becky nodded.

'Then why don't you get vocal and tell me?'

'I can't!'

'Of course you can. And you can tell me what you want me to do as well…' Her panties were still on. He could breathe in her musky scent through them and see the dampness of her desire, a patch of moisture against the pale pink cotton. He didn't pull them down. Instead, he gently peeled them to one side, exposing her, and blew softly against the mound.

'What should I do next?' he enquired.

'Theo…' Becky gasped in a strangled voice. She'd slipped a little down the chair.

'Tell me,' he ordered softly. 'Want me to lick you down there? Want to feel my tongue sliding in and teasing you?'

'Yes,' Becky whispered.

'Then give me some orders…' He was so hot for her, turned on by her shyness, which was so different from what he was accustomed to.

He had to shed his clothes. Urgently. The top, then the jogging bottoms, taking his boxer shorts with them. She was looking at him, eyes wide.

'Lick me…' Just saying that made her whole body burn. 'I'm so wet for you…' He was so beautiful that he took her breath away. Her mind had always drawn a convenient line at the bedroom door. In her head, the act of making love stopped with kissing, fumbling and whispering of sweet nothings.

She had never pictured the reality of the naked male, not really. This surpassed all her fantasies and she knew, somewhere deep down inside, that the benchmark he had set would never be reached by any other man. He was so gloriously masculine, his body so lean and exquisitely perfect, the burnished gold of his colouring so impossibly sexy.

Theo pulled off the panties, wanting to take his time, and knowing that it would require super-human control to do that, because he was so hard he was hurting. She was wonderfully wet and she shuddered as he slid his questing tongue against her, seeking out the little throbbing bud and then teasing it, feeling it swell and tighten.

Becky was on fire, burning up. Two of his fingers joined his tongue in its devastating assault on her senses.

She pushed his head harder against her. She felt so ready to take him into her. 'Come in me,' she begged.

'All in good time.' Theo barely recognised his voice. Having boasted about his formidable talent for exercising control all the time in all areas of his life, he was finding out what it felt like to lose it. He was free-falling, his body doing its own thing, refusing to listen to his head…

Head buried between her legs, he sucked hard and felt her come against his mouth, her body arching up, stiffening, her breath sucked in as her orgasm ripped through her, long and shuddering.

He rose up, watching her brightly flushed face and her feverish twisting as her orgasm subsided.

His good intentions to hang onto his self-control had disappeared faster than water being sucked down a plug hole.

'Hold me,' he commanded, legs straddled over her.

Dazed, Becky took him in her hand. Nothing had ever felt so good. Every inhibition she had ever had when she had thought about making love to a man for the first time disappeared the minute he touched her.

It felt *so right*.

He made her feel special, made it feel natural for her to open herself up to him in the most intimate way imaginable.

Touching him now, she was no longer apprehensive, even though her mind skittered away from the physical dynamics of having someone as big as he was inside her. She was so wet and so giddy for him that it wasn't going to be a problem…

She delicately traced her tongue along his rigid shaft then took him into her mouth and felt a surge of heady power as he groaned and arched back.

Instinct came naturally. She even knew when he was

nearing his orgasm…and she sensed that this was not how he had planned things to go.

Looking down at her, Theo could scarcely believe that his control had slipped so completely that he couldn't contain the orgasm he knew was a whisper away. Her mouth circling him was mind-blowingly erotic, as was the focused expression on her face and the slight trembling of her fingers cupping him.

Intent on not coming like *this*, he pulled away, and for a second he thought that he had succeeded, thought that he could hold himself in check for the length of time it would take them both to get upstairs. He was mistaken. He could no more control the inexorable orgasm that had been building from the moment she had looked at him with those turquoise eyes…the moment he had known that they would end up in bed together, whether it made sense or not, whether it was a good idea or not…than he could have controlled a fast approaching tsunami.

For Becky, still transported to another planet, this was inexplicably satisfying because it was proof positive that he was as out of control as she was.

Watching him come over her had rendered her almost faint with excitement. Her heated gaze met his and his mouth quirked crookedly.

'Would you believe me if I told you that this has never happened in my life before?' Theo was still breathing thickly and still shocked at his body's unexpected rebellion. 'I'm taking you upstairs before it happens again.' He lifted her up in one easy movement and took the stairs quickly. She could have been as light as a feather. Her hair was all over the place, her cheeks were bright with hectic colour and her eyes drowsy with desire.

The curtains hadn't been drawn and weak moonlight seeped into her bedroom. It was still snowing, a steady, silent fall of white that somehow enhanced the peculiar dream-like feel to what was going on.

Theo took a few seconds to look at her on the bed. Her dark hair was spread across the pillows and her pale, rounded body was a work of art. Her breasts were big, bigger than a generous handful, her nipples cherry-pink discs.

He was going to take his time.

He'd acted the horny teenager once and it wasn't going to happen again. He still couldn't compute how it had happened in the first place.

He joined her on the bed, pinned her hands to her side and straddled her.

'This time,' he said roughly, 'I'm going to take my time enjoying you…' He started with her breasts, working his way to them via her soft shoulders, down to the generous dip of her cleavage, nuzzling the heavy crease beneath her breasts until he settled on a nipple, and there he stayed, lathing it with his mouth, suckling, teasing and tasting, drawing the throbbing, stiffened bud into his mouth, greedy for her.

Becky writhed and groaned. She spread her legs and wrapped them around him, desperate to press herself against the hardness of his thigh so that she could relieve some of the sensitivity between them. But he wasn't having that and he manoeuvred her so that she was lying flat, enduring the sweet torment of his mouth all over her breasts.

He reached back to rub between her legs with the flat of his hand but not too much, not too hard and not for long.

He needed more than this erotic foreplay. He needed to be inside her, to feel that wetness all around him.

'My wallet's in my bedroom,' he whispered hoarsely. 'I need it to get protection. Don't go anywhere…'

Where was she going to go? Her body physically missed his for the half a minute it took for him to return and, during that time, she thought again about whether she should tell him the truth, tell him that she was a virgin…and, just as before, she quailed at the thought.

But as he applied the condom, looking directly at her as his fingers slid expertly along his huge shaft, she felt a twinge of nerves.

Theo settled between her legs and nudged her, pushing against her wetness gently. He wasn't going to go hard and fast. He was going to take his time and enjoy every second of her. He felt her momentarily tense but thought nothing of it. He was so fired up he could barely think at all and he certainly couldn't read anything from her response until he pushed into her, sinking deep and moving faster than he wanted but knowing that he just had to.

He heard her soft grunt of discomfort and stilled. 'I'm a big boy…tell me if I'm hurting you because you're really tight. Deliciously tight…' He sank deep into her and then it clicked.

Her blushing shyness, the way he had felt, as though everything he was doing was being done for the first time, that momentary wince…

'Bloody hell, Becky—tell me you're not a virgin…?'

'Take me, Theo. Please don't stop…'

He should have withdrawn but he couldn't. *A virgin.* His body was aflame at the thought. He'd never wanted any woman the way he wanted this one. Every sensation running through his body felt primitive. He was the caveman he never thought he could be, and the fact of her virginity made him feel even more primal, even more like a caveman.

Their bodies were slick with perspiration. With a groan, he thrust hard, deep into her tightness, and the feeling was indescribable as she rocked with him, wrapping her legs around his waist and coming seconds before he did, crying out as she raked her fingers along his back, the rhythm of her body matching his.

'You should have said.' He fell onto his back, disposing of the condom and thinking that he should be feeling a lot more alarmed that he had slept with someone as innocent as she was. So much for her escape to the country in the wake of some dastardly affair with a married man, or whoever it had been.

He was her first.

He'd never been more turned on.

'It doesn't make any difference.' She rolled so that she was half-balancing on his chest and staring down at him. 'Like I said, Theo, this isn't the beginning of anything for me. One night and then we exit one another's lives for ever…' She traced her finger around his flat, brown nipple. Why did it hurt when she said that?

'In that case…' Theo wasn't going to play mind games with himself as to whether he had done the right thing or not. 'Let's make the most of the night…'

CHAPTER FOUR

THEO STROLLED THROUGH into the kitchen of his sprawling four-bedroom penthouse and ignored the food that had been lavishly prepared by his personal chef, who kept him fed when he was in the country and actually in his apartment. The dish, with its silver dome, was on the counter, alongside a selection of condiments and some basic instructions on heating.

Instead, he headed straight for the cupboard, took down a squat whisky glass and proceeded to pour himself a stiff drink.

He needed it.

His mother, still in Italy, was back in hospital.

'A fall,' her sister Flora had told him when she had called less than an hour ago. 'She was on her way to get something to drink.' She had sounded vague and unsettled. 'And she tripped. You know those tiles, Theo, they can be very smooth and slippery. And I have told your mother a thousand times never to wear those stupid bedroom slippers when she is in the house! Those slippers with the fur and the suede are for your little box houses in England with lots of carpet! Not for nice tiles!'

'On her way to get something to drink?' Theo had picked up on the uneasy tone of his aunt's voice, and he had been right to, even though it had taken some prodding and nudging in the right direction to get answers out of her.

Now he sank into the long cream leather sofa and stared, frowning, past the stunning art originals on either side of the marble fireplace at nothing in particular. His mind was consumed by the very fundamental question...

What was he going to do?

His mother had not been on the way to fetch herself a glass of orange juice at a little after three-thirty in the afternoon. Nor had she tripped in her haste to make herself a fortifying cup of tea.

'She has been a little depressed,' Flora had admitted reluctantly. 'You know how it is, Theo. She likes it out here but she sees me...my grandchildren...I cannot hide any of this from Marita! I cannot put my children and my grandchildren in a cupboard and lock them away because my sister might find it upsetting!'

Theo had gritted his teeth and moved the grudging conversation along, to discover that depression was linked with drinking. His mother had gradually, over the weeks, become fond of a tipple or two before dinner and it seemed that the tipple or two had crept earlier and earlier up the day until she was having a drink with lunch and after lunch.

'Why haven't you told me this before?' he had asked coldly, but that had produced a flurry of indignant protests and Theo had been forced to concede that Flora had had a point. She didn't share the villa with his mother. She would not really have seen the steady progression of the problem until something happened to bring it to her notice.

Such as the fall.

'She's due out of hospital in a week's time,' Flora had said. 'But she doesn't want to return to London. She says that she has nothing there. She enjoys my grandchildren, Theo, even though it pains her to know that...'

There had been no need for his aunt to complete the sentence with all its barely concealed criticism.

Getting married and having hordes of children was the Italian way.

Going out with legions of unsuitable women, remaining stubbornly single and promising no grandchildren whatsoever was not.

And it wasn't as though he had siblings who could provide for his mother what he was unwilling to.

But he had to do *something*...

He glanced at his computer, lodged on the gleaming glass table on which he had stuck his feet. For a few seconds, he stopped thinking about the predicament with his mother and returned to what he had spent the last fortnight thinking about.

Becky.

The woman had occupied his mind so much that he hadn't been able to focus at work. The one night, as it happened, had turned into three because the snow had continued to fall, a wall of white locking them into a little bubble where, for a window in time, he had been someone else.

He had stopped being the powerhouse in charge of his own personal empire. He had stopped being responsible for all those people who depended on him for a livelihood. There'd been no fawning women trying to get his attention wherever he went or heads of companies trying to woo him into a deal of some sort or another. He was untroubled by the constant ringing of his mobile phone because service had been so limited that, after informing his PA that he couldn't get adequate reception, he had done the unthinkable and switched the phone off.

He had shed the billionaire persona just as he had shed the expensive clothes he had travelled in.

He had chopped wood, did his best to clear snow and fixed things around the house that had needed fixing.

And of course he had noted all the flaws with the cottage, which were not limited to the leaking roof. Everywhere he'd looked, things needed doing, and those things would only get worse as time went on.

He knew that if he played his cards right he would be able to get the place at a knockdown price. He could bypass her altogether. He had found out where her parents lived, even knew what they did for a living. He could simply have returned to London, picked up the phone and made them an offer they couldn't refuse. Judging from the state of the cottage, it wouldn't have had to be a high offer.

But that thought had not even occurred to him. He had played fast and loose with the truth when Becky had first asked him what had brought him to the Cotswolds and, like all good lies, it had been impossible to disconnect from it.

Maybe he had kidded himself that once he returned to London his usual ruthlessness would supplant his momentary lapse in character when he had been living with her. It hadn't worked that way and he had spent the past fortnight wondering what his next step was to be.

And, worse, wondering why he couldn't stop thinking about her. Thinking about her body, warm, soft and welcoming. Thinking about the way she laughed, the way she slid her eyes over to him, still shy even though they had touched each other everywhere. She haunted his dreams and wreaked havoc with his levels of concentration but he knew that there was no point picking up the phone and calling her because what they had enjoyed had not been destined to last.

They had both recognised that.

She had laughed when he had stood by her front door, back in his expensive cashmere, which was a little worse for wear thanks to the weather.

'Who *are* you?' she had teased, with a catch in her voice. 'I don't recognise the person standing in front of me!'

'It's been fun,' he had returned with a crooked smile but that about summed it up.

Back in the clothes she usually didn't step out of, she was the country vet, already thickly bundled up to go to the practice where she worked. He could no more have transported her to his world than he could have continued in her father's old clothes clearing snow and chopping wood for the fire.

But he'd felt something, something brief and piercing tugging deep inside him, a sharp ache that had taken him by surprise.

He focused now and looked around him at the fabulous penthouse, the very best that money could buy. He'd bought it three years previously and since then it had more than quadrupled in price. It sat at the top of an impressive converted glass and red brick government building which was formidably austere on the outside but outstandingly modern and well-appointed on the inside. Theo liked that. It gave him the pleasant illusion of living in a building of historic interest without having to endure any of the physical inconveniences that came with buildings of historic interest.

He wondered how Becky would fit in here. Not well. He wondered how she would fit into his lifestyle. Likewise, not well. He moved in circles where the women were either clothes horses, draped on the arms of very, very rich men, or else older, at ease with their wealth, often condescending to those without but in a terribly well-mannered and polite way.

And the women all dripped gold and diamonds, and were either chauffeured to and from their luxury destinations or else drove natty little sports cars.

But his mother...would like her. She was just the sort of natural girl his mother approved of. There was even something vaguely Italian about the way she looked, with her long, dark hair and her rounded, hourglass figure.

His mother would approve and so...

For the first time since he had returned to London after his sojourn in the back of beyond, Theo felt a weight lift from his shoulders.

Trying to deal with the annoying business of Becky playing on his mind when she should have been relegated to the past had interrupted the smooth running of his life and he could see now that he had been looking at things from the wrong angle.

He should have realised that there was only one reason why he hadn't been able to get her out of his mind. She was unfinished business. The time to cut short their sexual liaison had not yet come to its natural conclusion, hence he was still wrapped up with her and with thoughts of making love to her again.

He would make contact with her and see her again and he would take her to see his mother in Italy. She would be a tonic for his mother, who would be able at least to contemplate her son going out with a woman who wasn't completely and utterly inappropriate.

She would find her mojo once again and, when she was back to full strength, he would break the news that he and Becky were finished, but by then Marita

Rushing would be back on her feet and able to see a way forward.

And, he thought with even greater satisfaction, she would have the cottage to look forward to, the cottage she had wanted. Would Becky agree to speak to her parents about selling it to him? Yes. She would because it made financial sense and he had no doubt that he would be able to persuade her to see that. The house was falling down and would be beyond the point of reasonable sale in under a year, at which point the family home would either collapse into the ground or else be picked apart and sold to some developer with his eye on a housing estate.

Would she agree to this little game of pretend for the sake of his mother's health? Yes, she would, because that was the sort of girl she was. Caring, empathetic. When she had spoken about some of the animals she had treated in the course of her career, her eyes had welled up.

The various loose strands of this scheme began to weave and mesh in his mind.

And he felt good about all of it. He was solution-oriented and he felt good at seeing a way forward to solving the situation with his mother, or at least dealing with it in a way that could conceivably have a positive outcome.

And he felt great about seeing Becky again. In fact, he felt on top of the world.

He nudged his mobile phone into life and dialled…

Becky heard the buzz of her phone as she was about to climb into bed, and she literally couldn't believe her bad luck, because she had had two call-outs the past two nights and she really, *really* needed to get some sleep.

But then she drowsily glanced at the screen, saw who was calling and her heart instantly accelerated into fifth gear.

He had her number. He had taken it when he had been leaving on that last day because the roads had still been treacherous, even though the snow had lightened considerably, and she had been worried about him driving to London in his *silly little boy-racer car.*

'I'll call you if I end up in a ditch somewhere,' he had drawled, and then he had taken her number.

Noticeably, he hadn't given her his, and that had stung, even though she had made it perfectly clear that what they'd had was a done deal—there for the duration of the snow, and going just as the snow would go, disappearing into nothing until you couldn't even remember what it had been like to have it there.

Of course he hadn't called but for her the memory of him hadn't disappeared like the snow. Where white fields had faded from her mind, the memory of him was still as powerful after two weeks as it had been after two hours.

It didn't help either that, with the practice winding down, work was thinning out as the farmers, dog-owners, cat-owners and even one parrot-owner began transferring business to the nearest practice fifteen miles away. She had the feeling of being the last person at the party, hanging around after the crowd had dispersed when the lights were being switched on and the workers were beginning to clear the tables. The same sad, redundant feeling of someone who has outstayed their welcome.

And the house...

Becky had decided that she wouldn't think about the house until she had found herself a new job because there were only so many things one person could worry about.

But neither of those massive anxieties could eclipse the thoughts of Theo, which had lodged in her head and continued to occupy far too much space. She found herself regularly drifting off into dreamland. She wondered what he was doing. She longed to hear his voice. She checked her phone obsessively and then gave herself little lectures about being stupid because they had both agreed that theirs would only be a passing fling. She rehearsed fictional conversations with him, should they ever accidentally bump into one another, which was so unlikely it was frankly laughable.

She wondered why he had managed to get to her the way he had. Was it because he had come along at a point in time when she had been feeling especially vulnerable? With her job about to disappear and her sister finally achieving the picture-postcard life with her much-wanted baby on the way? Or was it because she had been starved of male attention for way too long? Or maybe it had been neither of those things.

Maybe she had never stood a chance because he was just so unbelievably good-looking and unbelievably sexy and she had just not had the arsenal to deal with his impact.

When she caught herself thinking that, she always and inevitably started thinking about the women he might now be seeing. She hadn't even asked him whether he had a girlfriend! He had seemed, for all his good looks, as the honourable sort of guy who would never have cheated on any woman he might have been seeing, but of course she could have been wrong.

He could have returned to London in his fancy car and immediately picked back up where he had left off with some gorgeous model type.

Realistically she had never expected him to get in touch so she stared open-mouthed at the buzzing mobile phone in her hand, too dumbstruck to do anything.

'Hello?'

Theo heard the hesitancy in her voice and immediately

knew that he had done the right thing in contacting her, had made the right decision. When he had driven away from her house two weeks ago, he had told himself that he had had a good time, but at the end of the day she had been a virgin and he'd been driving away from a potential problem. She had laughed off the fact that he had been the first man she had slept with, had told him that she was attracted to him, and why not?

'You're not the right guy for me,' she had said seriously. 'But, if I carry on waiting for Mr Right to come along, I might be waiting for a very long time.'

'In other words, you're using me!' he had laughed, amused, and she had laughed back.

'Are you hurt?' she had teased.

'I'll survive...'

And she hadn't been lying. There had been no clinging when the time had come for him to go. She hadn't tried to entice him into carrying on what they'd had. There had been no awkward questions asked about whether he would miss her. Her eyes hadn't misted over, her lips hadn't trembled and she hadn't clung to the lapels of his coat or given him one final, lingering kiss. She had smiled, waved goodbye and shut the door before he had had time to fire up the engine.

He might have been her first but he certainly wasn't going to be her last. Maybe that was another reason why he hadn't been able to get her out of his head. He'd effectively been dumped, and he'd never been dumped in his life before, simple as that.

'Becky...'

Becky heard that wonderful lazy drawl and the hairs on the back of her neck stood on end. She steeled herself to feel nothing, but curiosity was eating her up. Had he missed her? Had he been thinking about her every second of every minute, which was what it had felt like for her? Thinking about him all the time...

'How are you?'

'Been better.' They could spend time going around in polite circles before she asked him the obvious question—*why have you called?*—and Theo decided that he would skip the foreplay and get down to the main event. 'Becky, I could beat around the bush here, but the fact is I've called to ask you for...a favour. This would be a favour better asked face to face but...time is of the essence, I'm afraid. I just haven't got enough of it to woo you into helping me out.'

'A favour?' Of course he hadn't called because he'd missed her. Disappointment coursed through her, as bitter as bile.

'Do you remember I spoke to you about my mother? It would appear that...' He sighed heavily. 'Perhaps it would have been better to be having this conversation face to face after all. I know that this is asking a lot, Becky, but there have been some...unfortunate problems with my mother—problems that do not appear to have a straightforward solution.' The direct approach was failing. He stood up, paced and sat back down. 'I need you, Becky,' he said heavily.

'Need me to do what?' Her voice had cooled.

'Need you to come to London so that I can talk to you in person. I can send my driver for you.'

'Are you crazy, Theo? I don't know what's going on with your mother. I'm sorry if she's having problems but you can't just call me up out of the blue and expect me to jump to your summons.'

'I understand that what we had was... Look, I get it that, when you closed your front door, you didn't anticipate me getting in touch with you again.' Theo seriously found it hard to believe that this could actually be the case because the shoe was always on the other foot. Women were the ones desperate for him to make contact and he had always been the one keen to avoid doing any such thing.

He instinctively paused, waiting to hear whether she would refute that statement. She didn't.

Becky thought that he was certainly right on that count—she hadn't anticipated it—but she had hoped. It hadn't crossed her mind that she would indeed hear from him and he would be asking a favour of her!

That certainly put paid to any girlish illusions she might have had that their very brief fling had meant anything at all for him. She was thankful that she had waved him a cheery goodbye and not made any mention of hoping that they might meet again.

'You're right—I didn't—and I don't see how I could possibly do you any favours in connection with your mother. I don't even know her.'

'She fell,' Theo said bluntly. 'I've just come off the telephone with her sister. She apparently...' He paused, dealing with the unpalatable realisation that he was actually going to have to open up about a situation which felt intensely personal and which he instinctively thought should be kept to himself.

'Apparently what...?' Becky could feel vulnerability in his hesitation. He was so strong, so proud, so much the archetypal alpha male that any sort of personal confession would seem like an act of weakness to him.

Despite herself, she felt her heart go out to him, and then banked down that unwelcome tide of empathy.

'She's been depressed. The recovery we had all hoped for has been a physical success but...'

Again, that telling pause. She had a vivid picture of

him trying to find difficult words. She felt she knew him, and then she wondered how that was possible, considering they had spent a scant three days in one another's company. *Knowing* someone took a long time. It had taken her nearly two years before she had felt that she *knew* Freddy, and then it had turned out that she hadn't known him at all, so how likely was it that this sensation of being able to *sense* what Theo was feeling from down the end of a telephone was anything other than wishful thinking?

She wasn't going to give in to any misplaced feelings of sympathy. By nature, she was soft. It was why she had chosen to study veterinary science. Caring for sick and wounded animals was straight up her alley. But Theo was neither sick nor a wounded animal. He was a guy she had slept with who hadn't bothered to get in touch with her until now, when he obviously wanted something from her.

'She fell because she was drinking,' he said abruptly.

'Drinking?'

'No one knows how long it's been going on but it's reached a stage where she's drinking during the day and…a danger to herself. God knows what might have happened if she had been behind the wheel of a car…'

'I'm so sorry to hear that,' Becky said sincerely. 'You must be worried sick…'

'Which is why I called you. If my mother's problems are alcohol related, then it's obvious that she's slipping into a depressed frame of mind. There were signs of that happening before she left for Italy…' He sighed heavily. 'Perhaps I should have insisted that she go for therapy, for counselling of some sort, but of course I thought it was a straightforward case of being down because she had had a stroke, because she had had a brush with her own mortality.'

'That's understandable, Theo.' Becky automatically consoled him. 'I wouldn't beat myself up over it if I were you. Besides, there's nothing you can do about that now. Weren't you the person who made a big deal about telling me how important it was to live in the present because you can't worry over things that happened in the past which you can't change?'

'I told you that?'

'Over that tuna casserole you told me you hated.'

'Oh, yes. I remember...'

Becky's skin warmed. His voice had dropped to a husky drawl with just the ghost of a satisfied smile in it and she knew exactly what was going through his head.

He had pushed the dish of tuna bake to one side, pulled her towards him and they had made love in the kitchen. He had laid her on the table, her legs dangling, the dishes balanced in a heap that could have crashed to the floor at any given moment. He had parted her legs and had licked, sucked and nuzzled between them until she had been crying and whimpering for him to stop, for him to come inside her—and come inside her he had, with urgent, hungry, greedy force that had sent her soaring to an orgasm that had gone on and on and had left her shattered afterwards.

'So,' she said hurriedly, 'you couldn't have foreseen. Anyway, I'm sure everything will be fine when you bring her back to London, where you can keep an eye on her. You could even employ someone...'

She wondered whether that was the little favour he had phoned about. Perhaps he had returned to his busy tycoon lifestyle and was too preoccupied with making money to make time, so he'd decided that she might be able to see her way to helping him out. She'd been short-sighted enough to mention to him that the practice was going to close. Maybe he thought she'd have lots of free time on her hands.

'She's refusing to return to London.'

'Yes, well...'

'Nothing to come back here for, were, apparently—her words.'

'I still don't see why you've called me, Theo. I don't see how I could possibly help. Maybe you should...'

'Needs something to live for.'

'Yes, but...'

'She's old-fashioned, my mother. She wants what her sister has. She wants...a daughter-in-law.'

Becky thought she had misheard and then she figured that, even if she hadn't, she *still* had no idea what that had to do with her.

'Then you should get married,' she said crisply. 'I'm sure there would be hundreds of women falling over their feet to drag you up the altar.'

'But only one that fits the bill. You.'

Becky burst out laughing, manic, disbelieving laughter. 'You've telephoned out of the blue so that you can ask me to marry you because your mother's depressed?'

Theo's mouth compressed. He hadn't *asked her to marry him*. He loved his mother but even he could see a limit to the lengths he would go to in order to appease her. But, if he had, hysterical laughter would not have been the expected response.

'I'm asking you to go along with a fake engagement,' he gritted. 'A harmless pretence that would do wonders for my mother. We go to Italy...an all-expenses-paid holiday for you...and you smile a lot and then we leave. My mother will be delighted. She will have something to live for. Her depression will lift.'

'Until she discovers that it's all been a complete lie and there won't be any fairy-tale white wedding.'

'By which time two things will have been achieved. She will no longer be so depressed that she's dependent on a bottle to help her through, and she will realise that I'm capable of having a relationship with someone who isn't a bimbo.'

'So let me get this straight,' Becky said coldly. 'I'm the one for this *harmless pretence* because I have a brain and because—I'm reading between the lines here—I'm not tall, blonde and beautiful. I'm just an ordinary girl with an ordinary job so your mother will like me. Is that it?'

'You're not exactly what I would call *ordinary*,' Theo mused.

'No.' She was shaking with outrage and, underneath the outrage, hurt.

'Why not?'

'Why do you think, Theo? Because I'm not into deceiving people. Because I have some morals—'

'You're also heading for the unemployment line,' he said, cutting her off before she could carry on with her list of high-minded virtues. He was still scowling at her roar of laughter when she had thought he might have called to ask her to marry him. 'Not to mention living in a house that's falling apart at the seams.'

'Where are you going with this?'

'I could get you up and running with a practice of your own. You name the place and I'll provide the financial backing and cover all the advertising. In fact, I can do better than that—I'll set my team on it. And I'll get all those nasty little things that are wrong with your house repaired...'

'Are you trying to *buy* me so I do what you want?' And the weird thing was...she had thought about him so much, wanted him so much, would have picked up where they had left off if he had made the first move and called her. But this…

Theo wondered how his brilliant idea had managed to get derailed so easily. 'Not buying you, no,' he said heavily, shaking off the nasty feeling that yet again with this woman his self-control was not quite what it should be. 'Business transaction. You give me what I want and I give you…a great deal in return. Becky, that aside…' his voice dropped a notch or two '… I'm asking you from the bottom of my heart to do this for me. Please. You told me that you loved your parents. Put yourself in my shoes—I only want my mother to regain her strength.'

'It's not right, Theo.'

He heard the hesitation in her voice and breathed a heartfelt sigh of relief.

'I am begging you,' he told her seriously. 'And be assured that begging is something I never do.'

Becky closed her eyes tightly and took a deep breath. 'Okay. I'll do it, but on one condition…'

'Name it.'

'No sex. You want a business transaction, then a business transaction is what you'll get.'

CHAPTER FIVE

BECKY HAD WONDERED whether she would be given the fortnight off. She was owed it, had worked unpaid overtime for the past few months, but leaving someone in the lurch was not something she liked to do.

She had half-wished that she would be firmly told that she couldn't be spared, because as soon as she had agreed to Theo's crazy plan she had begun to see all the holes in it. On the contrary, her request was met with just the sort of kind-hearted sympathy that had made her realise how much she would miss working for the small practice.

'You come and go as you please until the place closes,' Norman had said warmly. 'Can't be nice for you, working here, knowing that it's winding down and that you won't be seeing our regulars again. Besides, you need to start thinking about your next job—and don't you worry about anything, Rebecca, you'll get a glowing reference from me.'

'The faster you can make it to London, the better, Becky,' Theo had said as soon as those fateful words— *okay, I agree*—had left her mouth, and he hadn't allowed her to sit on her decision and have any sort of rethink.

She'd needed a bit of time to get things sorted with her job and her house before she just breezed off abroad for two weeks.

'What things?' he had demanded.

She could practically hear him vibrating with impatience down the end of the line. He'd called her several times over the two-day period she'd taken to pack some stuff, check the house for incipient problems that might erupt the minute her back was turned and anxiously leave copious notes on some of the animals that had been booked in to have routine procedures done over the two-week period.

Already regretting her hasty decision, she'd plied him with questions about his mother.

She'd repeatedly told him that it was a crazy idea. He'd listened in polite silence and carried on as though she hadn't spoken, but he *had* talked about Marita Rushing and about the health problems that had afflicted her. He'd only closed up when she'd tried to unearth information prior to the stroke, to life before she had started worrying that her son might never marry and might never make her the grandmother she longed to be.

'Not relevant.' He swept aside her curiosity with the sort of arrogant dismissiveness that she recognised as part and parcel of his vibrant, restless personality.

'She won't believe that we have any kind of relationship,' Becky told him the night before she was due to leave for London. Ever since she had laid down the 'no sex' ground rules, he had been silent on the subject. He hadn't objected and she'd thought that he was probably glad that she had spared him the necessity of trying to resurrect an attraction that hadn't lasted beyond her front door.

That hurt but she told herself that it simplified things. He had suggested that she treat his proposition as a business transaction, and there was no reputable business transaction on the planet that included sex on tap. They'd had their fling and now this was something else. This was his way of doing the best he could to try and get his mother back on her feet and her way of trying to sort out her future.

In a way, accepting his generosity almost turned it into a job—an extremely well-paid job, but a job nevertheless—which meant she could distance herself from that flux of muddled emotions she still seemed to have for him.

It helped her to pretend to herself that there wasn't a big part of her that was excited at the prospect of seeing him again.

'People always believe what they want to believe, but we'll talk about that when you come,' he eventually said.

Becky had accepted that. She'd had too much on her mind to pay attention to whatever story line he might think up. He insisted on sending a driver for her, even though she had told him that the train was perfectly okay.

Now, sitting in the back seat of his chauffeur-driven black Range Rover, she felt the doubts and hesitations begin to pile up.

Along with a suffocating sense of heightened tension, which she valiantly tried to ignore. She told herself that he was not going to be as she remembered. She was looking back at that small window in time through rose-tinted specs. He wouldn't be as striking or as addictive as she had found him when he had stayed with her. Locked away in the cottage with the snow falling outside, she had built their brief fling into an impossibly romantic tryst.

The fact that they were so unsuitable for one another had only intensified the thrill. It was like putting the prissy, well-behaved head girl in the company of the bad boy who had roared into town on his motorbike. No matter how much the sparks might fly, it would all come crashing down because it wasn't reality.

When she went to London, reality would assert itself and she would see him as he really was. Not some tall, dark, dangerously sexy stranger who had burst into her humdrum life like an unexploded bomb, but a nice-looking businessman who wore suits and ties and carried a briefcase.

He would be hassled-looking, with worry lines on his face that she hadn't noticed because she had been swept away on a tide of novelty and adventure.

He hadn't been lying about his wealth. He'd never boasted, but he hadn't tried to hide it. She'd briefly wondered whether he had been enticing her by exaggerating just how much punch he packed, but any such vague doubts were put to rest as the silent, über-luxurious car pushed through the London traffic to glide into a part of the city that was so quiet it *breathed* wealth.

The tree-lined street announced its pedigree with the cars neatly parked outside fabulous, very pristine mansions. Some had driveways, most didn't. At the end of the street, a severe, imposing building dominated the cul-de-sac. It was gated, with a guard in a booth acting as sentry just within the ornate black wrought-iron gates. The very fact that the place was secured against anyone uninvited was an indication of the sort of people who lived there and her mouth fell open as the car drove through, directly to an underground car park.

Becky tugged her coat around her and thought about the two worn, battered cases she had brought with her. She hoped no one would see her on her way to his apartment because she would probably be evicted on the spot.

He had come into her world and he had slotted in, had replaced his city garb with her dad's country clothes and had mucked in as though he had spent his entire life in a shambolic cottage in the middle of nowhere.

But that was not his world. This was. And there was no way that she was going to fit in with the sort of seamless ease with which he had fitted into her world.

'I'll show you to the underground lift.' The chauffeur turned to glance at her. It was the first thing he had said since a polite 'Good morning' earlier when he had greeted her at the front door and taken her cases from her to stick them in the car trunk.

Becky nodded and they walked, in silence, through some glass doors into a reception area which housed a bank of four gleaming lifts, comfortable furniture for several people to relax and two very big, very well-cared-for plants that formed a feature on either side of the row of lifts. Yet another guard in uniform was sitting behind a circular desk and he nodded and exchanged a few pleasantries with Theo's driver, who had brought her bags out with him from the car.

This had all been a very bad idea. She should never have come. She didn't belong here. Their worlds had collided and then flown off in different directions. She should have left it there, just an exciting memory to draw upon now and again, something to put a smile on her face as her life, temporarily upset, carried on along its prescribed route.

Instead, she was here, listening to the porter tell her where to locate Theo, who would be waiting for her. Her battered bags were by her feet. She felt cumbersome and ungainly in her big coat, with all its useful pockets, and underneath the big coat there was nothing more glamorous. Her usual jeans, layers and baggy jumper. She wondered what the chauffeur had thought of her, and now she wondered what the porter was making of her, but she refused to give in to all the insecurities nudging at the door.

This was a business deal. She was doing him a favour and he was doing her one. There was no necessity for her to fit in or not fit in.

But her stomach was knotted with nerves as she was whooshed up in the mirrored lift to the fourteenth floor.

The lift opened out onto a plush carpeted landing. She stared straight ahead into an oversized mirror, on either side of which were two grand abstract paintings.

'Turn right,' the porter told her with a kindly smile, 'and you can't miss Mr Rushing's apartment.'

She turned right and saw the porter had not been kidding. The entire floor was clearly occupied by just one apartment. The corridor was more of an outside landing, with a glass and metal sideboard against the wall over which was another abstract work of art. It was very light and airy. She looked around her and just then, just as she was torn between moving forward and fleeing back to the sanctuary of the lift, a door opened and there he was.

Her heart fluttered erratically and her mouth went dry. He hadn't changed and it had been absurd wishful thinking to have hoped that he might. If anything, he was taller, more aggressively masculine and more sinfully sexy than she remembered. Wearing loafers, a pair of black jeans and a black, fitted short-sleeved polo, he was lounging against the doorframe, watching her as she tried to get herself together and present a composed image.

Theo looked at her. His mind, coolly analytical, recognised what he had known would present itself to him and that was a woman who, quite simply, didn't fit into the world of sophistication and glamour he occupied. He had known that she wouldn't have dressed for the occasion, and anyway, he doubted she had the sort of clothes that would allow her to blend in. She looked ill at ease, with her ancient suitcases on either side of her, and in the exceptionally practical sort of outfit that worked when she was tearing off to see to a sick animal but offered nothing more than functionality.

But then there was that other part of him...the part that remained uncontrolled by his coolly analytical mind... the part that had made him lose concentration at work because he hadn't been able to get her out of his mind...

The part that looked at her standing metres away from him and felt a surge in his libido that took his breath away. It didn't matter what she wore, how unfashionable her clothes were or how awkward she looked as she hovered suspiciously by her cases... She still turned him on.

But no sex.

Those had been her ground rules, and of course they made sense. It didn't matter whether he still wanted her or not. It had been short-sighted to imagine furthering what they had had by a fortnight so that he could somehow get her out of his system.

Perhaps if she had jumped at the opportunity to get back into bed with him again...

If she had greeted his phone call with the sort of breathless pleasure with which any other woman would have responded...

Well, under those circumstances, he would have had no problem in stepping up to the plate and taking what was on offer. But, if she had been the sort of woman to agree to two weeks of abandoned sex, then she wouldn't have been the woman he had gone to bed with.

She might have fancied him, she might have lost her virginity to him because she had been unable to fight the attraction and at that point in her life had chosen to allow the physical side of her to overrule the intellectual side of her, but essentially he wasn't the type of man she was interested in—hence the 'no sex' stipulation.

Common sense had reasserted itself. Of course, she was right. She was far too serious to indulge in a no-strings-attached liaison, especially when she would be going against the grain and faking a relationship with him for the sake of his mother.

The most important thing was his mother's health and he didn't want Becky to start questioning what she was doing because they were sleeping together, because she was having an affair with the wrong guy.

Besides, he had never chased any woman, and he wasn't about to start now.

Annoyed with himself because his libido wasn't playing ball, he pushed off from the doorframe and walked towards her. She looked as though, given half a chance, she would turn tail and scarper.

But of course she wouldn't do that, would she? She was being paid for the favour she was doing him. It didn't matter how morally high-minded you were, money always ruled the day.

She'd only been persuaded into this escapade because of the money. He had thought her different from all the other women he had ever dated in the past, women who had been impressed by his bank balance and the things he was capable of buying for them, but was she really?

His mouth thinned. At least the cards were on the table with no grey areas for misunderstandings. This was a business transaction and focusing on that would get his wayward libido back on the straight and narrow...

'You're here.' He picked up her bags and stood back, silver-grey eyes skirting over her. 'I wondered if you'd get cold feet at the last minute.'

Becky heard the cool in his voice and interpreted it as

what it was—the voice of a man who no longer had any physical interest in her. He needed her help and he was willing to pay a high price for it. This wasn't about any lingering attraction or affection on his part. This was about business and she shouldn't be surprised because, when it came to business, he was clearly at the top of the field and you didn't get there without ruthlessly being able to take advantage of opportunities.

He wanted to do what he felt was the best thing for his mother and she was an opportunity he had taken advantage of.

'I was tempted.' Becky fell into step alongside him and decided right there and then that she would have to be as cool and as detached as he was. 'But then I thought about what was on the table and I realised that I would be a fool to turn down your offer.'

'You mean the money.' His voice hardened as he stood back, allowing her to brush past him into the apartment.

Becky slipped past and was frozen to the spot. This wasn't an *apartment*...this was a *penthouse complex*. It was very open plan. Staring ahead, she looked at the wall of raw brick interrupted by a series of modern paintings that she knew, without being clued up on art, were priceless originals. Curving to the left was a short, twisting spiral staircase that led to an arrangement of rooms which she assumed to be bedrooms, although she could be wrong. But there were living spaces in front and on either side, from the glorious, huge sitting area with its white arrangement of leather sofas to a spacious kitchen in shades of grey and a dining area that was cool and contemporary. There were almost no walls, so the spaces all ebbed and flowed into one another in a beguiling mix of brick, wood and marble.

And it was vast. High ceilings, limitless space and

cool, subdued colours that always seemed to character-ise immensely expensive houses. This was the sort of place where too much colour would be a rude intrusion and clutter was to be discouraged at all costs.

'Impressed?' Against his will, Theo felt a kick of pride at her awed expression. Other women had been awed. Frankly, all of them. This one was different.

'It's beautiful.' Becky turned to him, her glorious eyes sincere. 'You must feel very privileged living here...'

Theo shrugged. 'I've stopped noticing my surround-ings,' he said, sweeping up the cases and striding off to-wards the staircase. 'Just as you, doubtless, have stopped noticing the leaking roof in your cottage.' Part of the deal had been to do repair work on the cottage, and Theo in-tended to do a damn good job so that the basics could be covered before he bought the place, because he had no doubt that it would be his in due course, especially now that setting her up in a practice of her own was part of the deal.

He wondered what it would be like to set her up with a practice in London...

Then he shook free the ridiculous notion.

'I'm not allowed to forget the leaking roof,' Becky said coldly, 'considering I have to avoid stepping in a bucket of water every other day.'

'Had it fixed yet?' He paused outside a bedroom door to look down at her.

Becky stared back up at him, angry with herself for the way he could still make her feel like this—hot, bothered and unsteady—when obviously everything had changed between them. She had to get a grip. She couldn't spend the next two weeks in a state of heightened awareness.

'One of my friends has offered to oversee the repair

work. I didn't think I could leave it leaking and unsupervised for two weeks.'

'I'll cover the costs.'

'There's no need.'

Theo pushed open the bedroom door but then stood in front of her, barring her path. 'Let's not skirt away from the base line here, Becky. There's a deal on the table and I intend to stick to it. You're doing me a great favour, and in return you get repair work done to your house and I set you up in a practice of your own so that you don't have to worry about whether you'll be able to get another job easily or not.'

Becky reddened. Put like that, without all the frilly business of helping him out to soften the *base line*, she couldn't quite believe what she was doing here. The practical side of this had not been the real reason she had ended up here, had it? It appalled and frightened her, if she was being brutally honest with herself, but she knew that the bigger part of her reason for standing right here, in front of a bedroom in this marvellous penthouse suite of rooms, was because she had nurtured the tiniest slither of hope that he might still find her as attractive now as he had a fortnight ago. She had broken all her rules when she had slept with him. It hadn't mattered how inappropriate he was for any kind of relationship, she had wanted to keep on breaking those rules for a little bit longer.

Now that she was here, it seemed like a ridiculous thing ever to have thought. She stuck out like a sore thumb and she wouldn't be surprised if he made sure to hide her away until they disappeared off to Italy, just in case he was spotted by anyone he knew.

Of course he wouldn't fancy her. Of course she had been a blip for him, just as he had been a blip for her. He would never have got in touch had the unfortunate situation with his mother not arisen. Thank goodness she had not shown her hand but instead had gone on the defensive the minute she had realised that he wanted her to do him a favour, and had laid down her 'no sex' ground rules. She knew that if he had chosen to break them, declared that he had missed her after all, then she would have cracked. She knew that if he had looked at her when she had stood there in that plush landing and then swept her up into his arms, her 'no sex' stipulation would have crumbled.

It hadn't happened and she had been an idiot to think that it might have.

'Fine.' She smiled brightly and peered around him to the bedroom which, like the rest of the place, was the last word in fabulous. 'Would you mind very much if I… er…had a shower? It's been a long drive down here…'

She risked a quick glance. She wanted to ask him why he was in a mood with her when he had been the one to ask her down here in the first place, but she didn't, because she needed to be as cool as he was. She wasn't going to start pleading with him to be *friendly*. Maybe he resented having her here in the first place. Maybe he felt as though he had been cornered into doing the only thing he could think of for his mother but, really, he didn't want to. He just didn't have a choice. Perhaps he had wanted to get back to his normal life of playing with beautiful, glamorous models but suddenly he had had to rummage up a feasible girlfriend to produce to his mother and she had been the only woman he knew plain enough to pass muster.

'And then,' she carried on, 'we could hammer out the details? If I'm supposed to be involved with you, we should at least get our stories straight.'

Theo marvelled at the speed with which she had abandoned her scruples about deceiving his mother and fallen in line now that there was a financial incentive dangling on the horizon.

'Quite,' he drawled. Her bags looked lost and out of place where he had placed them and he clenched his jaw, toughening up against any weakness inside him to imagine that those bags were a reflection of their owner, who must also be feeling lost and out of place.

'I...' She turned to him, burying her hands in her pockets so that she didn't impulsively and foolishly reach out to touch him. 'I've never done anything like this before...' She shuffled and then made herself stop, reminded herself that she was a qualified vet who dealt with far more important situations than this and handled herself competently and efficiently.

'Which is why we have to discuss what's going to happen. It's not going to be believable if you're a bag of nerves whenever you're around me. My mother will want to believe that I'm actually capable of being attracted to a woman with a brain, but even she is going to start having doubts if you act as though you're terrified of slipping up. Anyway, take your time, I'll be downstairs in the kitchen. We can...discuss how we proceed when you join me.'

He felt he needed a stiff drink.

By the time she emerged forty-five minutes later, he was wondering what exactly the details of his little ill-conceived adventure might be. His mother knew that he was bringing a girl to meet her and had already perked up because this was the first time in nearly two years he had done that.

There was no going back now.

His cool eyes swept over her as she slowly walked into the kitchen. She had changed into jeans and yet another baggy jumper and was wearing a pair of bedroom slippers.

Becky didn't miss the way he had given her the once-over and yet again she was burningly conscious of just not fitting in to the surroundings, a bit like a cheap souvenir from a package holiday amidst a collection of priceless pieces of china.

You didn't seem to mind this look when you were in my cottage, she thought with sudden resentment.

'You're doing it again,' Theo drawled, strolling to get a glass from the cupboard and pouring her some wine.

'Doing what?'

'Looking as though you'd rather be anywhere else but where you actually happen to be.'

'This is just such a stupid idea.'

'I suggest you move on from that. It's too late to get cold feet now and, besides, you have nothing to worry about.' He drained his glass and poured another. It was a little after seven and food had been prepared by his chef. From nowhere came the memory of her little kitchen and the way he would sit at her kitchen table, watching her as she cooked, anticipating touching her.

'What do you mean *I have nothing to worry about*?' She gulped down some wine and looked at him cautiously. He was just so beautiful. Why couldn't her imagination have been playing tricks on her?

'It's going to be two weeks,' Theo said drily. 'Two weeks for which you will be richly rewarded. In return, all you have to do is smile prettily and chat now and again. I will be with you at all times. I'm not asking you to turn into my mother's best friend. Your main purpose will be to...' he sighed heavily '...give her a purpose, make her see the future as something to look forward to.

It's a short-term plan,' he continued with a hint of dissatisfaction, 'but it's the only plan I have.'

'Why don't you just take someone you actually want to have a proper relationship with?' Becky suggested, frowning. 'Instead of this great big charade?'

Theo burst out laughing. 'If I had one of those stashed up my sleeve,' he mused, 'then don't you think I would have pulled her out by now? No, if I were to present my mother with any of the women from my little black book, she would run screaming in horror. She's had her fill of my women over the years. I honestly don't think her heart could take any more.'

'Why do you go out with them if they're so unsuitable?'

'Whoever said that they were unsuitable *for me*?' Theo answered smoothly. 'At any rate, it's irrelevant. Even if there was someone whose services I could avail myself of, it would be an unworkable arrangement.'

'Why?' Becky wondered whether he was actually aware of how insulting his remarks were.

'Because it would lead to all sorts of complications.' He thought of some of his girlfriends who had started daydreaming about rings and white dresses even though he had always made it clear from the outset that neither would be on the agenda. 'They might start blurring the line between fact and fiction.'

'How do you know that *I* won't do that?' Becky surprised herself by asking the question but this was a level playing field. He could say what he wanted, without any regard for her feelings, so why should she tiptoe round what she had to say to *him*?

'Because,' he countered silkily, 'you made it clear from the start that I wasn't your type and I don't see you getting any unfortunate ideas into your head.' She'd never told him what had driven her into the Cotswolds, what heartbreak had made her want to bury herself in the middle of nowhere. He wondered what the guy had been like. Nice, he concluded. So *nice* that he hadn't had the balls to entice her between the sheets. He couldn't stop a swell of pure, masculine satisfaction that *not nice* had done the trick.

'You're here because I offered you a deal you couldn't refuse and that suits me fine. No misunderstandings, no demands springing from nowhere, no unrealistic ambitions.'

And no sex... That could only be a good thing when it came to those nasty misunderstandings... Besides, if he had been having uninvited fantasies about her, then surely seeing her out of context, awkward and ill at ease in his territory as she was now, would slowly prove to him that her novelty value had been her only powerful draw...?

At the moment, he was still finding it difficult to look at her without mentally stripping her of her clothes, which was infuriating.

'But cutting to the chase...' He looked at the food which had been prepared earlier and was neatly in copper pans on the hob. He switched on the hob and had a quick think to ascertain the location of the plates. 'We met...?'

Becky shrugged. 'Why lie? Tell your mother where I live and that we met at my cottage. Tell her that you got lost because of the snow and ended up staying over for a few days.'

'That won't work,' Theo said sharply. He flushed and cursed the lie that could not now be retracted. 'Love at first sight might be a bit improbable.'

'Why?'

'Because it's not in my psyche, and anyone who knows me at all would know that.'

'So what *is* in your psyche?' Somehow, she had been so engrossed talking to him, that food had found its way to a plate and was now in front of her. Delicious, simple food, a fish casserole and some broad beans. With her nerves all over the place, her appetite should have deserted her, but it hadn't. The food was divine and she dug in with gusto.

Theo watched her, absently enjoying her lack of restraint. 'We met one another. After a diet of tall, thin models, beautiful but intellectually unchallenging, I fell, without even realising it, in love with someone who had a brain and made me jump through hoops to get her.'

Becky felt slow, hot colour invade her cheeks because, in that low, sexy, husky voice, it could have truly been a declaration of love. 'You mean you went for someone short and fat.' She covered over her embarrassment with a high-pitched, self-deprecating laugh and Theo frowned.

'Don't run yourself down,' he said gruffly. For a moment, he was weirdly disconcerted, but he recovered quickly and continued with cool speculation, 'There's no way I would ever have gone for someone who didn't like herself...'

'I like myself,' Becky muttered, glaring.

Theo grinned. 'Good. You should. Tall, thin and glamorous is definitely not all it's cracked up to be.'

Becky blushed, confused, because there was a flirtatious undercurrent to his voice, which she must have misheard because there had certainly been nothing flirtatious in his manner since she had arrived.

'And there's something else my mother would never buy,' he said slowly, pushing his plate to one side and relaxing back in the chair, his hands clasped behind his head so that he was looking down at her.

'What?'

'Your wardrobe.'

'I beg your pardon?'

'You can't show up in clothes you would wear on a house visit to see to a sick dog. You're going to have to lose the jeans and practical footwear. We're going to be staying on the coast, anyway. Much warmer than it is over here. You'll have to bid farewell to the jumpers, Becky, and the layers.'

'This is *me*,' she protested furiously. 'Aren't you supposed to have fallen for completely the opposite of the models you've always gone out with?'

'I'm not asking you to buy clothes that could be folded to the size of handkerchiefs but, if we're going to do this, then we're going to do it right. You'll have an unlimited budget to buy whatever you want...but it's time to kiss sweet goodbye to what you've brought with you...'

CHAPTER SIX

THEO GLANCED AT his watch and eyed the suite of rooms which Becky had been inhabiting with a hint of impatience.

His driver was waiting to take them to his private jet and he'd now been waiting for twenty minutes. Theo was all in favour of a woman's right to be late, except Becky wasn't that type, so what the hell was keeping her?

The vague dissatisfaction that had been plaguing him for the past forty-eight hours kicked in with a vengeance and he scowled, debating whether he should go and bang on her door to hurry her along.

The fact was that he had seen precious little of her since she had arrived at his apartment. They had discussed the nuts and bolts of what they would be doing but she had firmly rejected his offer to accompany her to the shops to buy a replacement wardrobe. She didn't want to do it in the first place, she had mutinously maintained, and she certainly wasn't going to have him traipsing around in her wake telling her what she could or couldn't wear. It was bad enough that he wanted her to try and project a persona she didn't have.

She'd made it quite clear that her decision to go along with the charade was one she had almost immediately regretted, and he'd been left in no doubt that only the prospect of having an uncertain future sorted out was the impetus behind her act of generosity. In other words, she'd been drawn by the offer of financial assistance. He was, above all else, practical. He could appreciate her sensible approach. He was grateful for the fact that there were absolutely no misplaced feelings of wanting more than the lucrative deal he had offered her. So, sex was off the agenda? He certainly wouldn't be chasing her although it was highly ironic that they were no longer physically intimate when they were going to have to convince his mother that they were.

He caught himself thinking that it would have been a damned sight more convenient if they had just fallen into bed with one another, for they were supposed to be a loved-up item, and then was furious with himself because he knew that he was simply trying to justify his own weakness.

If he'd thought that seeing her out of her comfort zone, an awkward visitor to *his* world, would cure him of his galloping, unrestrained libido, then he had been mistaken.

He still felt that he had unfinished business with her and for once his cool, detached, analytical brain refused to master the more primitive side of him that *wanted her*.

Had she brought a uniform of shapeless jumpers and faded jeans in a targeted attempt to ensure that he didn't try and make a pass?

Had she honestly thought that he would have forgotten what that body had felt like under his fingers?

He had become a victim of intense sexual frustration and he loathed it.

He wondered what she had bought to take to Italy and had already resigned himself to the possibility that she had just added to her supply of woefully unfashionable clothes as a protest against being told by him what to do.

Yet he had meant what he had told her...his mother knew him well enough to know that he liked well-dressed women. Or at least, she knew that the well-dressed woman was the sort of woman he was accustomed to dating. She'd certainly met enough of them over the years to have had that opinion well and truly cemented in her head. He might be able to sell her an intelligent woman as the woman who had finally won through but, intelligent or not, she'd never be convinced by a woman who couldn't give a damn about her appearance.

So how would she react if Becky decided to turn up in jeans and a baggy tee shirt? Trainers? Or, worse, sturdy, flat, laced-up shoes suitable for tramping through fields?

And yet, as he had told her, no other woman could possibly do for the role. And he couldn't think of a single one who would have held his interest long enough for his mother or anyone with two eyes in their head to believe that he was actually *serious*.

He smiled wryly because his mother would have been very amused if she could only see him here now, hovering by the door, glancing at his watch, prisoner of an unpredictable woman who wasn't interested in impressing him.

He was scrolling through messages on his phone when he became aware that she had emerged into the open-plan living area where he had now been tapping his feet for the past forty minutes.

He didn't have to look up.

He was as aware of her stealthy approach just as a tiger was aware of the soft tread of a gazelle.

He glanced up.

The battered bags, which he had insisted she replaced, were, of course, still there.

CATHY WILLIAMS 101

But everything else…

His eyes travelled the length of her, did a double take and then travelled the length of her all over again. He had been slouching against the wall. He now straightened. He knew that his mouth was hanging open but he had to make a big effort to close it because his entire nervous system seemed to have been rewired and had stopped obeying the commands from his brain.

Becky had had doubts about her drastic change of wardrobe. It had taken her far longer than necessary to get ready because she had wavered between wearing what she had bought and wearing what she was accustomed to wearing.

But he had got to her with those jibes about her clothes.

They had spent their glorious snatched time in the cottage snowed in, hanging around in old, comfy clothes. Because that was what the situation had demanded. But just how drab did he think she was? She had actually packed all of her summer wardrobe to take to Italy with her. She wasn't an idiot. She had known that thick layers would be inappropriate. How could he imagine that she would have presented herself as his so-called girlfriend dressed like a tramp?

She had never been more grateful for her decision to make sure he knew that the status of their relationship was purely business. If she had thought him not her type, then his stupid remarks about her having to change her appearance had consolidated that realisation.

How superficial was it to measure a woman's attractiveness by the type of clothes she wore?

But some devil inside her had decided to take him at his word. He wanted her to dress up like a doll? Then she would do it! She'd never been the sort to enjoying shopping. Buying clothes had always been a necessity rather than a source of pleasure. And in her line of work there was certainly no need to invest in anything other than purely functional wear. Durability over frivolity. She was all too aware that even the summer items she had packed were of a sensible nature. Flat sandals for proper walking in the countryside, sneakers, lightweight jeans and tee shirts in block colours, grey and navy, because bright colours had never been her thing. Her sister had always pulled off reds and yellows far more successfully.

But that was what Theo would be expecting. Perhaps even *dreading*. The fake girlfriend letting her side down by appearing like a pigeon to all the peacocks he had dated in the past. Maybe he had envisioned having to sit his mother down and persuade her to believe that he could actually fall for someone who didn't own a single mini-skirt and wouldn't have been caught dead wearing anything with sequins or glitter. Or lace, for that matter. And that included her underwear.

She had been timid in shop number one. Indeed, she had wondered what the point of being daring and rebellious was for a so-called liaison that wasn't destined to last longer than a fortnight.

But she had made herself go in and, by the time she had hit Harrods, she had found herself thoroughly enjoying the experience. How was it, she thought, that she had never sampled the carefree joy of trying on clothes, seeing herself as another person in a different light? How had she never realised that shedding her vet uniform could be downright liberating? She had retreated from trying to compete with her sister on the looks front and had pigeon-holed herself into the brainy bookworm with no time for playing silly dressing-up games. She had failed to see that there was a very healthy and very enjoyable middle ground.

In a vague way, as she had stood in one of the changing rooms, marvelling at the swirl of colour she had actually dared to try on, she had acknowledged that Theo was somehow responsible for this shift in her thinking. Just as he had been responsible, in a way, for hauling her out of her comfort zone, for taking her virginity, for being the one to make her enjoy the physical side of her.

Then she'd wondered what he would make of her change of wardrobe and that had spurred her on to be more daring than she might otherwise have been in colours, in styles, in shapes...

She'd even overhauled her lingerie, not that there had been any need, but why not?

And right now, in this breathless silence as he stood watching her with those amazing, brooding eyes, she thought that it had been worth every second of laborious trying on.

'I see you've gone for *barely there*...' Theo managed to get his legs working and his runaway brain back into gear.

The skirt was apricot and the top was dove-grey, and both fitted her like a glove, accentuating an hourglass figure that was the last word in sexy. The body that had driven him wild was on full display. Her tiny waist was clinched in, her full breasts were stunningly and lovingly outlined in the tight, stretchy top and even the grey trench-coat, which was as conventional as could be, seemed vaguely sensual because of the body it was incapable of covering up.

He'd told her that his mother would never have bought a girlfriend who dressed like a country vet, but he hadn't expected to be taken at his word.

And he didn't like it.

He scowled as he headed for her bags. 'I see you stuck to the ancient suitcases.'

'I thought it might be taking things a bit too far if I showed up with Louis Vuitton luggage considering I'm a working vet,' she snapped, stung by his lack of response to her outfit.

Would it be asking too much for him at least to acknowledge that she had done as asked and bought herself some peacock clothes?

Theo stood back and looked at her. 'No one would guess your profession from what you've got on.'

'Is that why you were staring at me?' she asked daringly. 'Because you think I should have bought stuff more in keeping with what a working vet on holiday would wear?'

They were outside and a driver was springing to open the passenger door for her.

Theo shot him a look of grim warning because he hadn't missed the man's eyes sliding surreptitiously over her, taking in her body in a quick sweep.

Harry had worked for him for two years and, as far as Theo could recall, had never so much as glanced at any of the women he had ferried from his apartment.

Theo flushed darkly. He turned to her as the car began purring away from the flash apartment block, through the impressive gates and in the direction of the airfield which, she had been told the day before, was an hour's drive away.

'When I suggested a change of wardrobe might be a good idea, I didn't think you'd go from one extreme to the other.'

'You said your mother would never find it credible that you would go out with someone who dressed the way I did. In other words, someone who looked like a bag lady.'

'That's quite the exaggeration.' But he had the grace to flush because she wasn't that far from the truth.

'You wanted me to be more like the kind of women you'd go out with so...' She shrugged.

Theo looked at her averted profile, the defensive tilt of her head, the way the skirt was riding provocatively up one thigh... He wondered whether she was wearing stockings or tights and his body responded enthusiastically to the direction of his thoughts.

'The women I'm accustomed to dating are...built a little differently to you,' he muttered truthfully. He had to shift to ease the pain of his sudden erection.

Becky's defences were instantly on red-hot alert but, before she could launch a counter attack, he continued, clearing his throat.

'They wouldn't be able to pull off an outfit like that quite like you're doing right now...'

'What do you mean?' Becky heard the husky breathlessness in her voice with dismay. This was a guy who had only got in touch because he had wanted something from her. A guy who had been happy to press on with his life after a couple of days. Even though she'd made a big deal of assuring him that there was no way he could ever have stayed the course with her, no way that she would want any more than the couple of days on offer, she'd be an idiot if she were to kid herself that she hadn't hoped for some sort of follow-up. Even a text to tell her that he missed her just a bit.

Because *she'd* missed *him* and thought about him a lot more after he'd gone than she should have.

She might not have played on his mind, but *he'd* played on *her* mind.

That had been part of the reason why she'd put down the 'no sex' rule when she'd agreed to his outrageous proposition.

If he thought that he could come to her for a favour,

tell her that she was the only one who fitted the bill because she was credibly average enough to convince his mother that he was serious about her, and then expect sex as some kind of bonus just because they'd been there before, then he was in for a shock!

But then, beneath that very sensible way of thinking was something she hardly dared admit even to herself. That *thing* she had felt for him and still felt for him after he'd disappeared back down to London frightened her. The power of his attraction had been so overwhelming that it had blitzed all her dearly held principles. In the face of it, she had had no choice but to throw herself into bed with him.

She was terrified that if she allowed herself to be weak, if she allowed herself to be overwhelmed by him again, then she would end up hurt and broken. She wasn't sure how she knew that but she just did.

So the last thing she should be doing right now was straying from the 'business arrangement' agenda and letting herself get side-tracked by personal asides.

'I mean…' he leaned towards her, his voice low '…my driver has never looked twice at any of the models who have stalked into this car over the years but he couldn't take his eyes off you.'

Becky went bright red. She wanted to put her hands to her cheeks to cool them. She glanced towards his driver, but the partition between the seats had been closed. Even so…

'If you think the stuff I bought is inappropriate, then I can easily, er, replace them…'

'Depends.'

'On what?'

'What else is in those suitcases of yours? Maybe I should have had a look before we left,' he continued in a low, thoughtful voice. 'Made sure you hadn't bought anything that would make my mother's hair curl...'

'You're being ridiculous,' Becky told him briskly. 'I doubt I've bought anything that any girl of my age wouldn't feel comfortable wearing, and your mother certainly wouldn't blink an eye at this outfit or any of the others if she's met any of your past girlfriends. I know, if they were all models, then what I'm wearing now would have been their idea of over-dressing.' Her skin was tingling all over and, although she wasn't looking at him, she was very much aware of his eyes on her, lazy and speculative.

Gazing at her pointedly averted profile, Theo had never felt such a surge of rampant desire. If this was what unfinished business felt like, then he wondered how he was going to cope for the next fortnight when he would be condemned to look without touching.

'At any rate, you've bought what you've bought,' Theo said roughly, dragging his mind off the prospect of trying to entice her into bed, because that would be a show of weakness he would never allow.

With the conversation abruptly closed down, Becky lapsed into nervous silence, while next to her Theo worked on his phone. When she glanced across, she could see him sending emails and scrolling through what appeared to be a mammoth report. He was completely oblivious to her. One minute it had felt so weird, so intimate...the next, she could have been invisible.

When she thought about the next fortnight, her stomach twisted into anxious knots, so instead she projected beyond that to where her life would be after they returned from Italy. He had told her that he would set her up in business, she only had to pick the spot, and she busied herself thinking about a possible location.

She wondered when the cottage would be sold. Her parents were unaware of the state of gradual disrepair into which it had fallen and that was something she had decided she would keep to herself. When it eventually sold—and there was no guarantee that would be soon, because the property market was hardly booming at the moment—it would get a far bigger price now that work was being done to fix the broken-down bits and she was pleased that her parents would reap the rewards from that. They had let her stay there for practically nothing.

Looking back at it, Becky could scarcely remember why she had felt so driven to run away when her sister and Freddy had tied the knot. She could scarcely remember what it had felt like to have a crush on Freddy or when, exactly, he had turned into just a pleasant guy who was perfect for her sister. She couldn't believe that some silly infatuation gone wrong had dictated her behaviour for years. If she hadn't allowed herself to lazily take the route of least resistance, she would not be here now, because she wouldn't have been at the cottage, pottering through life doing something she loved but without the necessary interaction with guys her own age.

She would never have met Theo. He had blasted into her life and galvanised her into really looking at the direction she had been taking. It just went to show how a series of coincidences could result in major life changes.

'Penny for them.'

Becky blinked and focused on him. He was leaning back against the door, his big body relaxed, legs spread slightly apart. Even like this, in repose, relaxed, he was the very image of the powerful alpha male and her heart gave a treacherous little leap.

'I was thinking about coincidences,' she said truthfully and Theo inclined his head.

'Explain.'

Becky hesitated. She knew that she needed to go on the defensive. She also knew that, if they were supposed to be *an item*, then for the duration of a fortnight she would have to stop treating him like the enemy.

He wasn't the enemy, she thought. Although he was... *dangerous*. Horribly, wonderfully, thrillingly, excitingly *dangerous*. And *that* was something she would never let on, because if there was one guy on the planet who would be tickled pink at being considered *dangerous* it was Theo Rushing. The more she agonised over the impact he still had on her, the more power she gave him over her state of mind.

He'd made those lazy little remarks to her about the way she looked and she'd practically gone into meltdown.

Well, it was going to be a nightmare if she went into a meltdown every time he turned his attention to her, especially considering they would have to pretend to be in love in front of his mother.

'I was thinking,' she ploughed on, determined to level the playing field between them so that she could be as cool as he was, 'that if you hadn't shown up out of the blue at the cottage, if it hadn't been snowing and you hadn't have ended up being stuck with me...'

'"Stuck" takes all the fun out of the memory.' Keen grey eyes noted the delicate colour that stained her cheeks and the way her eyelids fluttered as she breathed in sharply. Little giveaway signals that her 'no sex' rule had more holes in it than she probably would want to admit.

She'd made a big deal about how unsuited they were to one another and she was right. He could no more fall for someone as intensely romantic as she was than he could have climbed a mountain on roller skates. And, yet, the physical attraction was so strong that you could almost reach out and touch the electric charge between them.

She'd slept with him because she hadn't been able to fight that physical attraction. He hadn't been able to fight it either and he itched to touch her again.

Even though he knew that it probably wasn't a very good idea. He certainly wouldn't dream of going down the road of actively chasing her when a rebuff was waiting directly round the corner but...

He looked at her, eyes brooding and hooded.

There was no law against flirting, or pushing the barrier she had hastily erected, just to check and see how flimsy it was...was there...? Some might maintain that that would be a perfectly understandable response given that he was a red-blooded male with a more than healthy libido that just so happened to be fully operational when it came to her.

It would be a delicate compromise between maintaining his pride, holding on to his self-control and tipping his hat at common sense whilst testing the waters...and then playing a 'wait and see' game.

It would certainly enliven the next two weeks.

'I was drifting.' She ignored his little jibe. 'And you were a wake-up call.'

'Am I supposed to see a compliment in that?' he drawled. 'I don't think I've ever been described as any woman's *wake-up call*.'

'When this is over and done with, I feel that life can really start again for me.'

'I suggest we just get through the next couple of weeks before you start planning the rest of your life.'

'What if your mother doesn't like me?' Becky suddenly asked. 'I mean, you've taken it for granted that, because she hasn't approved of the women you've dated in the past, somehow she'll approve of me because I'm different from them—but she may not like me and, if she doesn't, then this whole charade will be a waste of time.'

Businesslike though this arrangement was, Theo was still irked to think that uppermost in her mind were worries about the financial side of things. 'Are you afraid,' he enquired coolly, 'That you might not get your money if things don't go according to plan?'

That had not occurred to Becky but she didn't refute it. She was going to be as cool about this as he was. She wasn't going to get bogged down in her own emotional issues. This was an exchange of favours and, the more she recognised that important aspect of their so-called relationship, the happier and more relaxed she would be. Their eyes met and she kept her stare as steady and as level as his.

'Well, nothing's been signed,' she pointed out with what she thought was an admirable amount of reasonable calm.

Theo gritted his teeth. One thing his mother was guaranteed to like about her was her honesty, he thought grimly. Marita Rushing had complained often and loudly that the bimbos she had met would have done whatever he asked because of his money.

'It must get boring for you,' she had declared a couple of years previously, after she had met one of the last of his leggy blondes before he had decided that introductions, always at his mother's insistence, were no longer a very good idea, however much she insisted.

His mother had never bought into the argument that having a woman do whatever he wanted was just what the doctor ordered for someone who had far too much stress on the work front to tolerate it on the home front. What he saw as soothing, she saw as unchallenging.

Becky took *challenging* to another level. If she didn't like anything else about his brand-new love interest, then that was something she would love. She would have first-hand insight into how frustrating the honest and challenging woman was capable of being.

By the end of the fortnight, he surmised that there was a good chance that his mother would be only too keen to concur when he'd say that there was a lot to be said for the eager-to-please lingerie model.

Instead of the woman who hadn't shied away from telling him that he wasn't her type, who had been frank about using him to please her, to teach her about making love, presumably so that she could implement the lessons learnt with a man more suitable... A woman who had agreed to help him out because of what she could get out of it in return and who, now, was worried that she might not reach the promised land if things did not go according to plan with his mother.

His lips thinned. 'Are you implying that I'm not a man of my word? That because I didn't get a lawyer to draw up an agreement for both parties to sign, that I would renege on what I promised to deliver?'

Becky sighed and lay back, eyes half-closed. 'You're the one who raised the subject.'

'Whatever the outcome of the next two weeks, you will get exactly what I have promised. In fact, name the place and I will get my people to start checking out suitable sites for a practice. Presumably you would want to go in with someone?'

She angled her head so that she was looking at him, and as always she had to fight not to respond outwardly to his masculine beauty.

'Maybe I'll go to France,' she thought aloud. 'Join the family. I'm going to be an aunt in a few months' time.'

And she wouldn't have a problem with Freddy. She could now, for the first time, fully admit what she had suspected for years. That, whilst she had been upset when he had chosen Alice over her, she hadn't been devastated. Whilst she had told herself that she needed to return to the family home, to be surrounded by what was familiar so that she could put heartbreak behind her, she had just given in to the indulgence of licking her wounds and then had stayed put because it had been easy. In truth, on the occasions when she had seen Freddy, she had secretly found him a little bland and boring—although to have admitted that, even to herself, would have opened up a Pandora's box of questions about the sort of man she was looking for.

She had always assumed that her soul mate would come in a package very much like Freddy's.

But Freddy was dull and so, she thought slowly, would be all those thoughtful, caring types she had held up as the perfect match for her.

She had allowed herself to assume, from a young age, that because Alice was the beautiful one in the family she would automatically be suited to guys as beautiful as she was. And for her, Becky, would come the steadier, more grounded, less beautiful types. But life had proved her very wrong, for her sister had fallen madly in love with the ordinary guy while she...

Her heart began to race. She felt nauseous, and suddenly she just couldn't look at the man next to her, even though she knew that she would still be able to see him with her eyes shut because he was so vividly remembered in her head. Like a diligent, top-of-the class student, the sort of student she had always been, she had filed away every single thing about him into her memory banks and all that information would now stay there a lifetime. She knew every small detail of his face, from the tiny lines that formed at the corners of his eyes when he smiled, to the slight dimple on just one side of his cheek when he laughed...from the way those silver-grey eyes could darken when he was roused, to the feel of his muscular shoulders under her fingertips.

She'd thought she was immune to him touching her heart because he hadn't ticked the right 'suitable for relationship' boxes in her head. She'd assumed that she hadn't been able to get him out of her mind after he had left for London because he had shaken her out of her comfort zone, so it was only natural that he had left behind a certain ache. What she hadn't done was ask herself the more fundamental question: why had she allowed him to break into her comfort zone in the first place?

Physical attraction was one thing but, of course, there had been much more to what she had felt for him, even after a day, two days...three days...

He had touched something deep inside her, stirred something into life. Why had no one warned her that love at first sight actually existed? Rather, why on earth hadn't she learnt from Alice and Freddy, both of whom had fallen head over heels in love from the very second their eyes had met?

And now here she was.

Panic and confusion tore through her. She felt she might faint. He was saying something about France, in that lazy, sexy voice of his but she barely heard him over the thundering of her heart. She wasn't aware of the car moving or didn't even know whether they were close to where his private jet would be waiting for them.

After a while, she heard herself responding to whatever he was saying. For the life of her, she had no idea what.

The only thing running through her head was the next two weeks and how she would survive them.

She could never let him suspect how she felt. She had her pride. If she had to live with memories, then she didn't want to add to the tally of difficult ones—the memory of him laughing incredulously at her or, maybe worse, backing away as if she were carrying a deadly infection.

The next two weeks weren't going to be a business arrangement to be endured as best as possible.

The next two weeks were going to be an assault course.

CHAPTER SEVEN

BECKY HAD GRUDGINGLY accepted Theo's advice that she change her wardrobe or risk not being a credible girlfriend. He was rich and he was accustomed to dating women for whom shopping for clothes was a career choice. Even if he liked women who didn't care, his definition of 'not caring' would be designer jeans and designer silk blouses and designer high heels, accompanied by lots of gold and diamond jewellery. Dressing down in a no-expense-spared kind of way.

There was no way cheap, durable, all-weather clothing would have passed muster.

One glance at his fabulous apartment had told her that. Her old, tired suitcases had stuck out in the midst of all the luxurious splendour of his penthouse apartment like an elephant in a china shop.

But his private jet—which, he explained with an indifferent wave of his hand, was useful to his CEOs for whom time was usually a great deal of money—was a sharp reminder not only why he had pushed her to buy a new wardrobe but of the huge chasm between them.

Even in her fancy, expensive clothes, she was horribly conscious of *not quite fitting in*. She knew that she was gaping. Gaping at the pale, soft, butter-cream leather seats and the gleaming chestnut interior. It was a small plane, fast and light, and capable of seating only a dozen people, but it was truly exquisite inside, with a long sideboard, on which was a basket heaped with fresh fruit, and a marble bathroom that included a shower and thick, fluffy towels.

Looking at her, Theo knew that he should have been put off by her obvious open-mouthed awe. She didn't pretend to be blasé about flying in a private jet. She was impressed and it was written all over her face. There was no need for her to say *wow* for him to notice that.

He wasn't put off. He was as pleased as the cat that had just got the cream. He dumped all intentions of working on the short flight and instead gave her an amused, verbal, in-depth description of the plane, what it was capable of doing and where he'd flown on business.

'You must have really felt as though you were slumming it when you got stuck in my cottage,' Becky said ruefully and Theo looked away.

The thought of admitting at this late stage that he had hardly found himself *stuck* in her cottage by pure chance was unthinkable. It hardly made a difference, because what did it matter whether she eventually found out or not that he had appeared there by design? But something inside him twisted, an uneasy tug on his conscience, which was usually unassailable.

'But you just fitted in,' she pondered absently.

'I didn't always have money at my disposal,' he said abruptly and she looked at him, surprised, because this was the first time he had ever come right out and said anything at all about his past. During all that concentrated time when they had been trapped in the cottage, held prisoner by the weather, he had talked about what he did, various situations he had encountered…he had amused her and held her spellbound with stories of the places he had been to...

But he had not once reminisced about his past.

'You act as though you were born with a silver spoon in your mouth,' Becky said encouragingly.

This was just *small talk*, she told herself. But deep down she already knew she had fallen in love with the man. She had recognised that awful, awful truth just as she had recognised that falling in love with him had not been part of the deal. But the deal was for her to keep up the act of being the woman he had recruited to play this role, the woman who wouldn't be stupid enough to try and blur fact with fiction, so shouldn't she be as natural and as chatty as she possibly could be?

And, if she learnt a little more about him, then where was the harm in that? She preferred not to think of it as furtively feeding her greedy desire to know as much about him as she could, to take as much as she was capable of taking with her, so that in the long weeks and months ahead she could pull all those little details out of their hiding places and dwell on them at her leisure.

'Do I?' Theo didn't know whether to be taken aback or amused at her blunt honesty.

'You don't pay any attention at all to your surroundings,' Becky explained. 'You barely notice all those wonderful paintings in your apartment and you hardly looked around you when you stepped aboard this jet.'

'It's easy to become accustomed to what you know. The novelty wears off after a while.'

'When did that happen?' Becky asked with lively interest. 'I'm only asking,' she hurried on, 'because, if we're supposed to be an item, it's only natural that I would know a little bit about you...'

'You know a great deal about me,' Theo drawled.

'But I don't know anything about your…past.'

'The past is irrelevant.'

'No, it's not,' Becky disagreed stoutly. 'The past makes us the people we are. What if your mother says something about you, expecting me to know what she's talking about, and I look at her blankly and have to admit that I haven't got a clue what she's talking about?'

'I doubt she'd die of shock,' Theo responded drily. 'I'm a private person and my mother is all too aware of that.'

'You wouldn't be private with someone you're supposedly serious about.'

'I think you're confusing me with someone else,' Theo responded wryly. 'You're mixing me up with one of those touchy-feely types who think that relationships are all about outpourings of emotion and the high drama sharing of confidences.'

'You're so sarcastic, Theo,' Becky muttered.

'Realistic,' Theo contradicted calmly. 'I don't do emotional drama and I wouldn't expect any woman I was serious about to do it either.'

Becky stared at him. 'You mean you'd want someone to be as cold and detached as you?'

'I wouldn't say that I'm *cold and detached*, and if you think hard about it, Becky, I'm pretty sure you'd agree.' He shot her a wolfish smile, enjoying the hectic colour that flooded her cheeks as she clocked what he was saying and bristled.

'That remark is inappropriate,' Becky spat, all hot and bothered. She had laid down her ground rules, and it was even more important now that he obey them, because how was she going to keep a clear head if he did again what he had just done? Got under her skin like that, with a few words and a sexy little smile?

'Why? Because you've told me that you're not interested in going to bed with me?'

Becky went from pink to scarlet. 'This—this isn't what this is about,' she stuttered, her voice letting her down because it was high-pitched and cracked, not at all the voice of someone cool, confident and in control.

'You shouldn't dress like that if you want me to stay focused,' Theo told her bluntly.

Becky hated the stab of pleasure that raced through her. She'd made the fatal error of thinking that sex was just an act that could be performed without the emotions coming into play. She wasn't built like that.

But Theo was.

He'd said so himself. He took women to bed and then dispatched them when they began to outstay their welcome. He never involved his emotions because he had no emotions to involve.

Emotional drama. That was what most normal people would call *falling in love* and it was what she had stupidly gone and done with the last man on the planet who deserved it. At least Freddy had been a worthwhile candidate when it came to feelings, even if she hadn't been the one for him nor, as it turned out, he for her. At least he was capable of *feeling.*

'If you recall,' Becky told him coldly, 'I was told that none of my clothes were going to cut the mustard...'

Theo grunted. He thought that it was a good thing that they would be staying at his villa. Fewer men crashing into lamp posts as they turned around to stare. His blood boiled when he thought of young Italian boys looking at her with that open, avid interest that they never bothered to hide. Salivating.

'Anyway.' She was keen to get away from the topic of her clothes, keen to get away from anything that could make her skin prickle and tease her body into remembering what it had felt like to be touched by him. 'You were filling me in on your background.' She smiled and cleared her throat. 'You were going to try and convince me that you remember what it's like to have no money when you act as though you were born to the high life. I can't believe you've ever been anything but rich...'

It occurred to Theo that it had been a long, long time since he had let his guard down with any woman. She was looking at him, her bright blue eyes soft and questioning, her full lips parted on a smile, her body language so damned appealing that he couldn't tear his eyes away from her.

'You're not trying to turn me into a touchy-feely guy, are you?' he murmured, but returned her smile.

'I wouldn't dream of trying,' Becky said honestly.

'Are you going to feel sorry for me if I tell you my sob story?'

'I don't believe you have a sob story.' Her heart was beating so fast and so hard, she could actually feel it knocking against her rib cage. This definitely wasn't flirting, they were having a proper conversation, but it still felt like flirting. There was still something charged in the atmosphere that made her tingle.

'My mother...had her heart broken when she was a young woman.' Theo was startled that he was telling her this because it was an intensely private part of his past that he had never revealed to anyone. 'I was very young at the time.'

'What happened?' Becky asked breathlessly.

'My father was killed. Quite suddenly. One of those freak accidents you read about sometimes. Wrong place, wrong time. My mother was inconsolable. She...' This was skating on thin ice, and he paused, but then decided to push on. Again, that tug on his conscience. Again, he swept it uncomfortably aside. 'Packed her bags overnight, from what I understand, sold for a song the house they had shared and went as far away as she could. Of course, there was no money. Or very little. She worked in all manner of jobs so that she could give me whatever she felt I wanted…or needed. She instilled in me the importance of education and made sure I got the best on offer. She worked her fingers to the bone because, in the midst of her own personal heartbreak, I was the only person in the world who mattered to her.'

And she'd never moved on. Until she'd started talking about the cottage, talking wistfully about her desire to return there after her hasty departure over two decades ago. Coming to terms with the tragedy that had broken her had, to Theo, been a signal of her moving on at long last because, if she could reconcile herself to the past, then she would be free of the vice-like grip it had had over her.

He'd preferred that *moving on* solution to the other, which was moving on to become a mother-in-law and eventually a grandmother, moving on to a different and more rewarding phase in her life.

'I can see why this is so important to you,' Becky said simply and it took Theo a couple of minutes to drag his mind away from the surprise of his confession so that he could properly focus on her.

'Have you been moved by my heart-breaking tale?'

'Don't be so cynical.' Did he feel that his duty from a young age had been to fulfil the role of man of the family? Had their lack of money made him thirsty for financial security? Her liberal-minded parents had prided themselves on their lack of absorption when it came to money. Was that why they had never told her that they might have liked the cottage to be sold so that they could have more of a financial comfort blanket? Having boxed themselves into the position of people who didn't place any value on money, had they then been too embarrassed to tell her to move out? Had that sentiment been there alongside the sympathy they had felt for her as the daughter with the non-existent love life?

She felt as though Theo had burst into her life and opened a Pandora's box of feelings and realisations she had never been aware of before.

'My mother will probably be a little subdued when we get to Italy,' Theo said, changing the conversation with a slight frown. 'My aunt will not have told her that she's made me aware of the reason for her hospital visit, which is good, but my mother is a proud woman, and I think she'll be nursing a certain amount of…shame that she has become reliant on alcohol to help her get through the day.'

'I get that,' Becky murmured.

There was nothing cloying about her sympathy and Theo slanted an appreciative glance across at her. She was matter-of-fact about the circumstances for this charade—a result of working in a profession where she was alert to all sorts of vulnerability in people, he guessed, who harboured deep feelings about the pets she was called upon to treat. A tough man might shed tears if his dog had to be put down but Theo guessed that those tears would only be shed in the presence of the vet who administered the final injection.

Becky decided that it was better not to dwell on Theo's surprising show of confidence-sharing. This wasn't some side of him he was unexpectedly revealing to her. This was necessary information he felt he had to impart and he had done so dispassionately.

Some gut instinct also made her realise that, if she

tried to reach out to him and prolong the moment, he would retreat faster than a speeding bullet and resent her for being the one with whom this very private information had had to be imparted.

She had never met a man more proud or more guarded. She could understand why the thought of having any one else do what she was doing had been out of the question as far as he was concerned. Any woman who was in the slightest bit interested in the sort of relationship he clearly had no interest in would have seized the opportunity to take advantage of his need to confide, would have seen it as an opportunity to go beyond the skin-deep experience he was willing to have.

Becky shuddered when she thought of the irony of sitting here, in love with him, if only he knew it.

Deliberately, she changed the subject, and it wasn't very long before the jet was dipping down to the landing strip and then gliding to a smooth stop.

They had left behind a cold and grey London—not freezing, as it had been in the Cotswolds, but nevertheless miserable and dank.

They landed here to blue skies and a crispness in the air that felt like the touch of perfect spring.

A car was waiting for them.

Theo might have had hard times growing up but he had certainly not been tainted by the memory. He had made his fortune and had no qualms in spending his money with lavish extravagance. No expense was spared when it came to creature comforts.

He led her to the waiting car and ushered her into the back seat, moving round to the opposite side so that he could slide in next to her.

'My mother grew up in Tuscany,' Theo told her as she stared out at the mouth-watering scenery flashing past them. Lush green mountains were the backdrop to picturesque, colourful houses nestled into the greenery like a child's painting of match boxes in different, flamboyant colours.

'But,' he continued, 'she moved to England when she met and married my father. When her own mother died six years ago, I decided to invest in a villa near Portofino, because that's where her sister lives. Of course, that was before the place became flooded with A-listers. I, personally, think they should have both moved back to Tuscany when Flora's husband died three years ago, but they like the weather on the peninsula.'

'Shh!'

'Come again?'

'Don't talk,' Becky breathed. 'It's interrupting my looking.'

Theo laughed and then gazed at her rapt expression as she took in the outstandingly postcard-pretty harbour dotted with fishing boats and luxury yachts and lined with tall, graceful, colour-washed houses.

A tantalising view before the car swept up into the hills, curving and turning so that flashes of the harbour appeared and disappeared, getting smaller and smaller with each brief glimpse.

Becky had forgotten all her doubts, her apprehension, even the stark, dangerous reality of her feelings for the man sitting next to her. All had been swept aside by the sumptuous glamour of her surroundings. She realised that she hadn't actually had a proper holiday in ages and certainly nothing along these lines. This was a one-off. She was dipping her toes into another world and it wouldn't happen again.

She caught her breath as the car glided smoothly through some impressive gates, up a tree-lined drive and then into a little courtyard, in front of which was a lovely two-storeyed house, gaily painted a bright shade of salmon, with deep-green shutters which had been flung back.

There were tall trees everywhere, casting patterns of shade across the walls of the house, and on the leafy grass and clusters of flowers, and bushes were pressed against the walls, seemingly trying to clamber upwards to the roof.

The porch on the ground floor was broad enough to house a cluster of chairs and its replica was a balcony on the first floor, the white railings of which were laced with foliage that spilled over the sides, bursting with colourful flowers that stretched down to reach the bushes and flowers that were clambering up.

It was enchanting and Becky stood still for a minute as the chauffeur and Theo, with the cases, walked towards the front door.

'Is this another *shh* moment?' Theo asked, strolling back for her and leading her gently to the door.

'I think I'm in love.' She looked up at him, face flushed, poised wickedly on a perilous ledge where she was telling him nothing but the complete truth, just for this heartbeat moment. 'With this beautiful house...' she completed with the thrill of someone who had just managed a narrow escape from the jaws of untold danger.

She was unaware of being observed until she heard some delighted clapping and, when she blinked and turned round, it was to see a small, very pretty middle-aged woman standing in the doorway of the house with a broad smile on her face. She was propped up and leaning heavily on a cane.

And in that split instant Becky saw with her own eyes the depth of love that had driven Theo to take the drastic measure of setting up this charade for the benefit of his mother.

For he had walked quickly to the door to sweep his mother into a hug that was uncharacteristically gentle and very, very loving.

'Enough of you!' Marita Rushing was tenderly pushing her way out of his bear hug to beam around him at Becky, who had remained in the background, dithering, acutely self-conscious and not quite knowing what to do.

'At last, he brings a *real* woman for me to meet! Come here and let me see you, child!'

'I haven't seen her this happy in a long time' was the first thing Theo said to her hours later, after Marita Rushing had retired for the evening to her quarters, which were on the ground floor—a very happy situation, considering her mobility was not yet back up to speed after the accident. It also meant that there was no concerned surprise that a bedroom wasn't being shared by the love birds. Marita Rushing might have been traditional but Becky didn't think that she was so traditional that she wouldn't have been suspicious to discover that her vastly experienced son was sleeping in a different bedroom from the love of his life.

Becky turned to him, half-wanting to continue the conversation, half-wanting him to leave, because he was in the room she had been allocated and she had yet to recover from all the touching that had gone on throughout the course of the evening.

'Don't forget,' he had whispered at one point, his breath warm against her ear, sending all sorts of forbidden tingles up and down her spine, 'that you're the light of my life, that I can't keep my hands off you...'

At that point, he had been sitting next to her on the

sofa whilst opposite them his mother had been chattering away, excitement stamped into every fluttering gesture and every thrilled smile. His hand had been on her thigh, casually resting there with the heavy weight of ownership. She had tried to snap her legs together but the insistent slide of his thumb at the very acceptable point just above her knee had prohibited any such display of prudishness.

They were an item and he had had no qualms about running away with the concept.

At every turn, she had felt those lazy grey eyes on her. When he had touched her, he had managed to touch her in places that provoked the greatest physical arousal, even though you'd never have guessed if you'd been looking from the outside, because every touch was as light as a feather and as soft as a whisper, lingering just a little too long and in places that were just a little too intimate.

'I'm surprised your mother wasn't a bit more curious as to the circumstances of our meeting.' She walked towards the window and looked outside to a moonlit night and the soft glow the moon cast on the silent, gently swaying trees and bushes. The window was open and she could breathe in the cool, salty tang of sea breeze. Beyond the lawns, trees and shrubbery, she could see the black, unmoving stillness of the sea, a different shade of darkness from the darkness of the sky. She could have gazed out at the scenery for ever, were it not for the presence of Theo, lounging by the door, sending ripples of awareness zinging through her body as lightning-fast as quicksilver.

She turned back around, perching against the window ledge, hands gripping the sill on either side of her. 'I mean…you happened upon an injured dog at the side of the road, whilst out driving in the country? And, concerned citizen that you are, you took it to the nearest vet who just happened to be me?'

Theo flushed darkly and frowned. Deceiving his mother did not come naturally to him. In fact, he had never deceived her about anything, not even about the unsuitable women who had liberally littered his life in the past. But the physical change he had seen in her was worth it. He hadn't been lying when he had said that it was the happiest he had ever seen her.

He wasn't about to let anyone climb on the moral high ground and start lecturing him about the rights and wrongs of the decision he had made when all that mattered, as far as he was concerned, was the end result. Least of all when that *someone* was a woman who was only in it for the money.

He quietly shut the door and walked towards her. She had changed from one sexy-as-hell outfit into another sexy-as-hell outfit. What surprised him wasn't his mother's lack of suspicion at the story he had told her, but her lack of suspicion at just how damned sexy a country vet could look.

But it wasn't just the way the soft, straight elbow-length dress in pale coral outlined the curves of her body. In itself, the dress hardly shrieked *sexy*...on anyone else it would just have looked like a pleasant, relatively expensive silk dress. But on *her*... Something about the shape of her body, the slightness of her waist, the soft flare of her hips, the shapeliness of her legs, combined with an air of startled innocence...

Just looking at her now was doing all sorts of things to his body. She was wearing a strapless bra. She was too generously endowed to go braless but, bra or no bra, it didn't take much for him to recall the sight of those cherry-tipped breasts and the way those cherry tips had tasted.

He raked his fingers through his hair and stopped abruptly in front of her, glaring into narrowed, bright blue eyes.

'Why would my mother question how we met?' he asked roughly, looking away, but then looking at her again and trying hard to resist the temptation to stare down at the contour of her body under the wispy dress.

'It just seemed a very unlikely story,' Becky muttered, folding her arms and sliding her eyes away from him.

'No more unlikely than some of my other introductions to women,' Theo muttered.

'Like what?'

'Three years ago I did a charity parachute jump from my jet and landed in a field where there was a shoot going on. Some butter advert. She was tall, blonde, Swedish and almost ended up flattened by me when I landed. We went out for nearly three months. Ingrid was her name.'

'And now here you are. With a country vet.'

'Like I said, I've never seen my mother happier.'

'Because she thinks that we're going to give her a happy-ever-after story,' Becky murmured, eyes cast down. She shuffled and then glanced up at him.

'I know what's going through your head, Becky. You think I'm being cruel because sooner or later she will discover that there will be no happy-ever-after...'

'Aren't you?' Before she had met his mother, Marita Rushing had been a name. Now she was a delightful, living, breathing woman, shrouded in sadness, but still ready to smile at the prospect of her son settling down. Deceit had never felt so immediate and yet she could still recall the way they had hugged and that feeling she had had that he was simply doing something he hoped would be for the best in the long run. 'Forget I said that.' She sighed. 'Do you have any plans as to how we fill our time while we're here?'

Theo had planned to work, whilst ensuring he cast a constant supervisory eye on Becky to make sure she kept her distance. He wanted his mother to like her, wanted her truly to believe that he was capable of forming relationships with girls who weren't five-minute visitors to his life because they were so utterly unsuitable. He wanted Marita to regain her strength so that he could bring her back to London. But he didn't want Becky to bond too firmly with his mother. After all, she wasn't going to be a permanent fixture in his life.

He also planned to have a word with his aunt to establish just what his mother's frame of mind was whilst she was recuperating at the villa.

And, lastly, he wanted to probe her about any potential interests his mother might have mentioned which he could weave into her life once she was in London.

There was still the matter of the cottage which, once bought, would be a welcome distraction from any brooding thoughts.

He frowned, recognising that the whole cottage-purchase scenario was mired in all sorts of ethical tangleweed. Something else he would see to when the time came.

For now...

'One step at a time' seemed the best way forward. First thing in the morning, he would check the cupboards to see what alcohol there was lurking. His mother had been restrained that evening, with just the one glass of wine. He needed to make sure that any drinking had been a temporary blip and not something that might require an intervention.

Work would have to take a back seat.

Between all the things he knew he would have to do, all the necessary obligations he would have to see to, a sudden thought threaded its way through, curving, cornering and bypassing duty, obligation and necessity, like a tenacious weed pushing past the well-laid rose bushes in search of light and air...

Time out.

Two weeks.

'There's a lot to see here,' he told her huskily. 'It's to be expected that we do some exploring.'

Becky looked at him in some alarm. 'Exploring?'

'That's what couples sometimes get up to when they go on holiday together,' Theo inserted.

'But we're not a couple,' Becky pointed out uneasily.

'Go with the flow, Becky.'

'That's easy for you to say.'

'Meaning?'

'Nothing.' She sighed, very nearly trapped by her own treacherous thoughts. It was easy for him to treat this like just some situation that could be enjoyed while it lasted. His emotions weren't involved. Hers were. A spot of sightseeing would be, for him, just a *spot of sightseeing.* Whilst, for her, it would be more sinking into the quagmire that was already engulfing her, making it almost impossible for her to stand back and take an objective view of what they were doing.

'And you're going to have to stop all that touching stuff,' she heard herself say in a burst of defiance.

She'd been thinking of how vulnerable it made her feel just being in his company. She'd been imagining what it would be like for them to be out and about, like a normal couple, doing something normal like sightseeing. Then she'd thought about him holding her hand and how that would feel, the sparks that would run through her—the stolen sensation of it *actually* being true, that they *actually* weren't playing a part...

She'd never thought that it would be possible to project so many scenarios into such a small space of time. Ten seconds and she had seen her life flash past straight into a black void of a future where every minute snatching stolen moments in the present would be weeks spent trying to find a way back to the light in the future.

And then she'd thought of him touching her, those devastating little touches that had meant nothing to him...

Now she just couldn't meet his eyes, because he would be wondering where that cool, collected woman had gone, the one who had agreed to go through with this because of the tangible rewards at the end of it. The one who had chatted to his mother as though the charade were no more difficult than anything else she had ever been called upon to do.

'What *touching stuff*?' Theo murmured in a low, husky voice.

'You know what I mean...' She looked at him with sullen defiance and he smiled, a slow, utterly mesmerising smile that made the breath hitch in her throat and brought her out in a panicked cold sweat.

'I haven't been touching you,' he said softly. 'This...' He trailed one long finger along her collar bone and then allowed it to dip under the neckline of the dress, before pausing at the dip between her breasts, in that shadowy cleavage that was rising and falling as though she were recovering from running a marathon. '*This* is touching you. I haven't been doing that, have I?'

'Theo, please...'

'I like that. I like it when you beg for me...'

'This isn't what it's about. This is...is...' His finger

had slipped deeper, was now trailing over the top of her strapless bra, making gentle inroads underneath, and she could feel her nipples poking painfully against the bra, wanting the thing he was teasing her with. 'This is a business arrangement,' she finished in a breathless whisper, shifting her body, but not nearly firmly or fast enough to avoid his devastating caress.

'I know, but I can't seem to take my eyes off you, Becky. And where my eyes go, my hands itch to follow...'

'You promised.'

'I did no such thing.' He stepped back with an obvious show of reluctance. 'If you don't want *that* kind of touching, then I'll refrain, but Becky—if you look at me with those hot little stolen looks, and you lick your lips like you'd love nothing better than to taste me, you can't expect me to keep my hands to myself.'

'I don't mean to do that!'

Theo dropped his eyes, appreciating the subtle message that way of phrasing her words had given him. She 'didn't mean to do that' implied that she was fighting to uphold the 'no sex' stipulation she had put on this little game of theirs, if it could be called a game. Which meant that she still wanted him as much as he still wanted her, but she was a good girl whose innate moral code could not permit random sex with a man with whom there would and never could be any future. She had succumbed once, and had probably used every argument under the sun to justify that weakness, but she was determined not to succumb again.

And he itched to touch her. He'd wanted it the second he'd decided to get in touch with her again and he hadn't stopped, even though he had his own inner voices urging caution.

Or at least urging him to pay some attention to his

pride…irritating little voices reminding him that he had never chased a woman in his life before and that there was no reason to start now. But he'd spent the entire evening fighting a war with a libido that was out of control…

'But you do it anyway,' he drawled softly. He held his hands up in a gesture of phoney surrender before shoving them into the pockets of his trousers. 'And, while you do that, don't expect me to play ball…'

CHAPTER EIGHT

TEN DAYS AFTER they arrived, Becky woke to the crippling pain of a headache, aching bones and the first, nasty taste of fever in her mouth.

And, for the first time in living memory, she thought that she might actually be *pleased* that she was about to come down with a cold. Or flu. Or any other virus that would give her an excuse to stick to her bed for twenty-four hours because the past few days had been the sweet-est of tortures.

Theo had laid his cards on the table. He wasn't going to play ball. She'd set her rules down and he'd coolly and calmly told her that he was going to ignore them.

So she had expected a full-on attack and had been bracing herself to deal with that. She had, as ammuni-tion, plentiful supplies of simmering anger, self-righteous moral preaching and offended outrage that he should dare to ignore *her* wishes.

If he wanted to stage an assault, then she would be more than ready for the fight, and she knew she would fight like a cornered rat, because her defences were fragile and her determination was weak and full of holes.

She was utterly and completely vulnerable to him and that, in itself, gave her the strength to cast him in the role of veritable enemy, which she felt was something she could deal with.

But there was no assault.

If anything, some of that intimate touching stopped. She would feel his eyes on her, a lazy, brooding caress that did all sorts of things to her senses, but those intrusive fingers on her skin when there was nothing she could do about it were no more. Indeed, after dinner, when they had fallen into the habit of sitting in one of the downstairs sitting rooms—an airy space where, with the windows flung open, the sound of the distant sea was a steady background roll—he would often sit opposite her, legs loosely spread, arms resting on his thighs, leaning forward in a way that was relaxed whilst still being aggressively alert.

Peeling her eyes away from him was proving a problem.

And, without her armour to fall back on, she had been reduced to playing a waiting game of her own which meant that she was always on full alert.

Several times she had asked him whether he might not like to escape and do some work.

'I'm perfectly happy to find a quiet corner somewhere and read,' she had told him. There were lots of those in the villa, although her favourite space was outside, curled up in a swinging chair on the veranda, from where she could see the stretch of front lawn with its shady trees and foliage and beyond that the flat ocean, a distant band of varying shades of blue.

'Don't you go worrying about me,' he had delivered in a soothing tone, although his eyes had been amused. 'It's delightful that you're concerned but, in actual fact, I'm managing to keep on top of my work very well at night.'

Which meant that the long days were spent in one another's company. They had had two trips into Portofino, where he had shown her around the picturesque harbour with its rows upon rows of colourful houses nestled in the embrace of the lush hills rising behind them. They had lunched at an exquisite and very quaint restaurant and she had had far too much ice-cold Chablis for her own good.

But his self-restraint had turned her into a bag of nerves and she had a sneaking suspicion that he knew that, which in turn made him all the more restrained.

For much of the time they were together, however, his mother was chaperone and companion.

For that, Becky was relieved because it afforded her a certain amount of distance from Marita Rushing. Becky knew, without a shadow of a doubt, that if she and the older woman were alone together for long enough they would become firm friends and the deceit in which she was engaged would feel even more uncomfortable than it already did.

She also suspected that Theo was deliberately making sure that he worked late at night, when everyone was asleep, so that he could keep a watchful eye on his mother, to ascertain her levels of alcohol intake.

'I honestly don't think she has a problem,' Becky had told him quietly the evening before, as they had been about to head off to their separate quarters.

'How would you know?' he had said roughly, but then had shaken his head, as though physically trying to clear it of negative thoughts. 'Are you a doctor?'

'Are you?' she had responded with alacrity. 'And, in actual fact, I have a great deal more training in medicine than you—and I'm telling you that there's no need to watch over your mother like a hawk. She hasn't said a word to you about the drinking situation because it was a blip on her horizon, and she's probably ashamed when she thinks about it now. If you keep following her around, she's going to begin to suspect that Flora has said something to you and she'll never live it down. She's a very proud woman.'

He had glowered but she had stood her ground and eventually he had laughed shortly and shrugged, which she had taken as a sign that he had at least listened to what she'd had to say.

But being with him all the time…was exhausting. She felt as though she couldn't drop her guard, even though she was beginning to wonder whether he hadn't lost complete interest in her after his cocky assertion that her defences were there to be knocked down should he so choose.

He might have wanted her to begin with but he wasn't a man who pursued and, in the end, old habits had died hard. She'd stuck her hands out to ward him away and he'd decided to back off because he couldn't be bothered to do otherwise.

And what really troubled her was the fact that *she cared.*

Instead of basking in the relief that she didn't have to keep swatting him away, she found herself missing that brief window when he had looked at her as though she still mattered to him, at least on a physical level.

She caught herself, on more than one occasion, leaning forward to get something, knowing that one glimpse and he would be able to see down her flimsy, lacy bra to her barely contained breasts.

So now she felt miserable with the start of a cold and she couldn't have been happier because she needed the time out to try and regroup.

An internal line had been installed in his mother's

room, connecting her to the kitchen and the sitting room, should she ever need to be connected, but in the absence of any such convenience Becky did the next best thing and dialled through to Theo's mobile.

She looked around her at the beautiful suite of rooms into which she had been put. Marita Rushing couldn't handle the stairs up, and there was no reason for her to venture up, but every day a housekeeper came and cleaned the house from top to bottom, as well as making sure that food was cooked, if that was necessary.

The housekeeper was a very quiet young girl who barely spoke a word of English and had been mortified, on day one, when Becky had helpfully tried to join her in tidying the bedroom.

At first Becky had wondered whether the girl would report back to Theo's mother that the loved-up couple slept in separate quarters, but then she very quickly realised that that would never happen.

Now, she wondered what it might have been like if that half-formulated, barely realised fear, which had been there when this whole charade had first been suggested, had actually come to pass. When Theo had first contacted her, she had quailed at the thought of having to share a bedroom with him, after the initial biting disappointment that the only reason he had picked the phone up had been to ask a favour of her.

For surely, in this day and age, that would be a given? If his mother was expected to fall for them being a couple, then she would likewise expect them to share a bed.

And what if they had?

Would her 'no sex' stipulation have been swept aside under the overwhelming surge of her physical attraction, combined with the power of knowing that she had fallen in love with him? Would common sense have been obliterated by the deadly combination of love and lust? Between those twin emotions, would there have been any room left for her head to prevail?

And would she have been worse off than she was now? Because she was a wreck. Which was probably why she had succumbed to a bug. Her body was telling her that she needed to rest.

Theo picked up on the third ring and, even though it wasn't yet six thirty in the morning, he sounded as bright-eyed and bushy-tailed as if he had been awake for hours.

'Why are you up so early?' were his opening words, and Becky nearly smiled, because for all the frustration he engendered in her she had become accustomed to certain traits of his. A complete lack of social niceties was one of those traits.

'Why are you?' she countered.

'Why do you think?' In the outer room, which had been converted into an office years previously—indeed as soon as the villa had been bought and the prospect of going there, even for a couple of days at a time, had become inevitable—Theo pushed himself away from the sleek, metal-and-wood desk and swivelled his chair so that he was staring out of the floor-to-ceiling window.

She hadn't come to him.

He'd really and honestly believed that she would have cracked. After all, he had seen the flare of mutual attraction in those luminous eyes, and he hadn't banked on her resistance, whatever she might have said to the contrary.

Why would he have? Since when had he ever been prepared to withstand any woman's resistance? He didn't know the rules of that particular game but he had felt his way and decided that he'd said what he had to say, but he wasn't going to push things with her. If she wanted to huff and puff and flounce around with maidenly virtue wrapped round her like a security blanket, then sooner or later she would drop the act.

He knew women, after all.

He also knew the power of good sex. It was more than a worthy adversary for any amount of doubts, hesitations or last minute qualms.

And they'd had good sex. The best.

Unfortunately he'd misread the situation and, having taken up a certain stance, he was condemned to dig his heels in or risk being a complete loser by being the first to crack.

It was beginning to do his head in. They were both bloody adults! They'd already slept together! It wasn't as though they were tiptoeing around one another in some kind of slow burn of a courtship game! Plus his mother was living the dream life, loving every second of seeing her son with a woman of whom she seriously approved.

Throw hot attraction into the mix and he just couldn't work out why it was that he was barely able to focus on his work and was having to take cold showers twice a day when it all should have been so simple.

And now, hearing her voice down the end of the line, he couldn't stop his imagination from doing all sorts of weird and wonderful things to his body as he pictured her, sleep-rumpled, in only her birthday suit.

Or else covered from top to toe in a Victorian maiden's nightie, to match her crazy 'no sex' rules...

Either image worked for him.

'I'm working.' He shifted, trying to release some of the sudden painful pressure.

'Do you *ever*,' she was distracted enough to ask, 'get any sleep at all, Theo?'

'I try and avoid sleep. It's a waste of valuable time.

Is that why you've called at…six forty in the morning? To check and see whether I'm getting my essential fix of beauty sleep?'

'I've called because…I'm afraid today is going to be a bit of a write-off for me.'

'Why? What are you talking about?'

'I've woken up with a crashing headache and all sorts of aches and pains. I think I may have a cold. It won't last but I'm going to stay in bed today.'

'My mother will be disappointed.' Theo stood up, brow furrowed. 'She had planned on introducing you to her favourite tea shop…'

'I'm sorry, Theo. I could venture downstairs but I feel absolutely rotten and I wouldn't want to…pass anything on to your mother. She's had a pretty poor year and a half and the last thing she needs is to catch germs from her house guest. In fact, if you don't mind, I'm going to grab some more sleep and hopefully I'll be fighting fit by tomorrow…'

'What have you taken?'

'Are you concerned?' Becky couldn't resist asking. 'Do you think that you won't be getting value for money if I take a day off?' As soon as the words had left her mouth, she wished that she could snatch them and stuff them back in.

'Are you offering to stay an extra day, Becky? I know you have a very strong work ethic.'

'I'm sorry. I shouldn't have… Well, I'm sorry…'

'Go back to sleep, Becky. I'll get Ana to bring you up some food when she gets here.'

He cut the connection, mouth thin as he contemplated the due reminder of why she was in this villa, mutual attraction or no mutual attraction. There was nothing like a sudden sucker-punch to remind a person of priorities.

* * *

Becky struggled up, reluctantly rising from a disturbed, fever-ridden sleep. She had taken a couple of tablets two hours previously and she could feel the effects of the tablets beginning to wear a little thin.

In fairness, she felt better than she had two hours before, but she still needed a day off, a day during which she could gather herself.

She didn't see Theo immediately. The curtains were drawn, thick, heavy-duty curtains designed to plunge the room into darkness so that if you wanted to lie in you weren't wakened by the stealthy creep of dawn's fingers infiltrating the room.

Sleepy eyes rested on the now familiar pieces of furniture, then shifted to the glass of water, now empty, on the side table, then...

'You're up.'

Becky's heart sped up and her mouth fell open, before a wash of misplaced propriety had her yank the sheet over her bare arms.

She had bought a complete new wardrobe and that complete new wardrobe included lingerie that she would never have dreamed of buying before. Little wisps of lace and not much else. Her nightwear was along those lines. It left next to nothing to the imagination. It couldn't have been more different from the homely, comfy, warm, practical nightwear she had made her own for the past twenty-seven years. She had thrown caution to the winds when she had gone on her shopping spree and had robustly decided, *in for a penny, in for a pound...*

'What are you doing here?' She was acutely conscious of her nipples scraping against the lacy top and the brevity of the matching knickers.

'Doctor's orders. Breakfast. I'm on a mission of mercy for the invalid. What would you like to eat?'

'Please don't put Ana to any trouble,' Becky begged. 'She has enough to do around here without bringing me up breakfast in bed as though I'm Lady Muck. I just need to spend the day in bed sleeping and I'll be back on my feet by tomorrow.'

'And, while you're in bed, the diet of choice for returning to full health is starvation? Because you don't want to put the housekeeper out?'

Becky flushed. Theo's attitude to the hired help was very different from hers. He was pleasant and polite but, as far as he was concerned, they were paid handsomely to do their jobs and were no different from any of the other employees in his service working at any of the companies he owned. A business transaction. Simple.

'Doesn't matter.' He waved one hand in nonchalant dismissal. 'Ana is off sick. Probably has the same bug that you have.'

'How awful!' Becky was stricken.

'And please,' Theo interjected with wry amusement, 'don't start beating yourself up about being the carrier of germs. I expect Ana brought it to the house with her. She has five siblings—a lot of scope for bugs to find places to set up camp.'

'And your mother? Don't tell me she has it as well…?'

'Fortunately not but I've shipped her off to Flora's for two days. Her health is fragile and the last thing she needs is a dose of the flu.'

'You're probably going to be next,' Becky said glumly.

'I'm never ill.'

'Have you told those germs that have set up camp with Ana's siblings? Because they might not know. They might have already decided that you'd make an excellent playground for them to have some fun on.'

'I'm as strong as an ox. Right. Food order.'

So it was just Theo in the house. There was no need for apprehension because, had he wanted to keep touching her and provoking her, he could have. All that had bitten the dust. His declaration of intent had been empty.

And now the poor guy felt obliged to put himself out for her when he would probably rather be working on a day off from supervising his mother and chaperoning his so-called girlfriend in the guise of enthusiastic lover.

'I guess...' she allowed her voice to linger thoughtfully before tailing off. 'I *guess* I should really have something to eat. I mean, I *have* had a pretty restless night, to be honest.'

Theo raised his eyebrows. The duvet had slipped a little and, if he wasn't mistaken, she didn't seem to be clad in the all-encompassing Victorian meringue he would have imagined. In fact, those thin spaghetti straps, as wispy as strands of pale cotton, pointed to a completely different get-up underneath the duvet.

'So what will it be?' he asked gruffly, clearing his throat and concentrating one hundred percent on her flushed face.

'Perhaps a poached egg,' Becky murmured. 'And some toast. Maybe a bit of fried ham as well, but not fried in oil, maybe fried in a little butter, just a dash. Protein. Important for my recovery, I imagine. And if there's juice... that would be nice. I noticed Ana squeezing oranges with an electric juicer... And perhaps some tea as well...'

'You've done a complete turnaround from not being hungry and not wanting to put anyone out,' Theo complained in a voice that told her that he knew very well what that turnaround was all about, and Becky smiled sweetly and apologetically at him.

'I'd understand if you didn't want to make me breakfast, Theo. I don't suppose it's the sort of thing you've ever done for any woman in your life before. In fact, I'm guessing that no woman would ever have been brave enough to have fallen ill when you were around to see it. They'd probably have known that they would get short shrift from you.'

'And that,' Theo countered smoothly, 'shows just how special you are, doesn't it? Because here I am, offering to be your slave while you're bedridden...'

Becky reddened. She knew why he was here. His mother would probably have told him to make sure he took care of her. Marita was like that. She had had a brief but idyllic married life with a man she had fallen desperately in love with at a very young age. Her concept of love was romantic and idealised because that was what she had had. She actually had no idea how jaded her son was when it came to the concept of love and romance. In her heart, she truly believed that he was capable of falling in love and finding the happiness she had found with her partner and soul mate.

Becky had come to understand exactly what Theo had meant when he had told her that, introduced to a girl deemed suitable, she would happily believe the fiction played out for her benefit.

She had also come to understand why he had done what he had because, however uncomfortable she was with the deceit, she could see improvements in his mother practically from one hour to the next. Flora, in a quiet aside two evenings previously, had confirmed how much Marita Rushing's frame of mind had improved since Theo had come to visit with Becky on his arm.

'She's a different woman,' Flora had confided. 'She is my sister again and not this poor, frail woman who felt she had nothing to live for... It was different when Theo was young and needed her, but since all those heart problems...and realising that he had no interest in settling down... Well, it is good that you are here.'

'I'm fine with just toast' was all she could find to say, mouth downturned at his coolness.

'I wouldn't dream of depriving you of essential sustenance to overcome your cold.' Theo grinned and gave her a mock salute. 'Anything else to add to the order? Or should I exit while the going's good?'

Becky allowed herself a smile once he'd left the room.

He got to her on so many fronts and one of those was his sense of humour. He could be as ironic as he could be cheeky and those two strands, woven together, was a killer package.

Reminding herself of the reality of their situation and the reality of what he felt for her was a daily challenge.

Lying back against the pillows, she wondered whether she should quickly change into something more suitable, but then realised that in her haste to replace her entire wardrobe for the two week period she had recklessly omitted anything that remotely resembled sensible clothing. Even the shorts she had packed had been knee-length linen. A small but exquisitely inappropriate wardrobe for someone who was now bedridden with a severe cold.

Theo returned less than twenty minutes later with a tray. He nudged the bedroom door open with his shoulder, half-expecting to find her sitting primly on the chair by the window, clad in anything but whatever sexy nightwear she had been wearing. However, she was still in bed, with the duvet sternly pressed flat under both arms, a step away from encasing her completely like a mummy.

'Your breakfast…' He dragged a chair over to the bed, deposited the tray on her lap and proceeded to sit down next to her.

'There's no need for you to stay.' Becky looked at the muddle of food on her plate and was puzzled as to how her poached egg and ham had been translated into something that was unidentifiable.

'The poached egg,' Theo pointed out with an elegant shrug, 'didn't quite go according to plan. I'm afraid I had to be creative…'

How could she keep the duvet in place while she ate? She tried, but gradually it slipped a little lower.

From his advantageous position next to the bed, Theo felt like a voyeur as he looked at the soft, silky smoothness of her shoulders and back. He talked to distract himself from falling into a trance because there was something hypnotic about the movement of her shoulder blades as she tucked into the breakfast.

Becky could feel those brooding, silver-grey eyes on her. Even though she wasn't looking at him, wasn't even sneaking sidelong glances in his direction…

Hot little looks, as he had called them…

The fever-induced weakness had been overtaken by a thrilling edge-of-precipice feeling as she finished the last morsel of food on the plate and dutifully put down her knife and fork.

When she glanced down, she could see how the duvet had slipped and how the lacy top was peeking open ever so slightly, allowing a fine view of her pale skin underneath.

This was playing with fire and she didn't know why she was doing that. She had spent so long being strong. She had accepted that he had lost interest in her. She had beaten herself up over her stupidity in falling in love with the man and had been extra careful to make sure that she wasn't exposed.

But now she could feel his eyes on her and that little voice that she had listened to right at the very beginning—that stupid little voice that had lured her to touch the flame, to climb into bed with him—was once again doing its thing and getting under her skin to wreak havoc with the defences she had meticulously been building up.

So, she'd fallen in love with him… So it had to be the most stupid thing she could ever have done…not that she had been able to stop herself… But here she was, fighting hard and being a martyr, making sure he didn't come near her. She'd given him her best 'hands off' stance, had told him that sex wouldn't be on the agenda, but, aside from feeling morally smug, what good had it done her? Was she happy and content with her decision? Had it made him any less tempting?

She was so desperate to read into the future and protect herself against further hurt—so keen to make sure he didn't add to the tally of pain she would suffer at a later date should she repeat her original mistake and get into bed again—that she was in danger of having a complete nervous meltdown.

'That was very nice. Thank you.' She heard the tell-tale throaty nervousness in her voice and glanced across at him as he removed the tray. When she leaned back against the pillows, she didn't rush to yank the duvet back up into position.

She feigned innocence, half-closing her eyes with a sigh of contentment at being well fed. She'd been hungrier than she'd thought and the eggy stuff he'd served up had been a lot tastier than she had expected.

She half-opened one eye to find him towering over her, arms folded, his dark features inscrutable.

He'd pulled back the curtains but not all the way and the sun penetrated the room in a band of light, leaving the remainder of the room in shadow. The light caught him at an angle, defining the sharp jut of his cheekbones and the curve of his sensuous mouth. He wasn't smiling. Nor was he scowling. He was…just looking, and adding things up in his head, and that sent a frisson of awareness racing up and down her spine, because she knew what things he was adding up and she liked that.

She'd missed him. He'd gone AWOL on her and she hadn't liked it. Her brain might have patted itself on the back and thought it'd won the battle but her body was staging a rebellion and common sense didn't stand a chance.

'You wouldn't happen to be playing any games with me, would you?' Theo asked softly.

'Don't know what you mean…'

'Oh, really, Becky,' Theo said drily. 'Would that be because you're just a poor invalid who's feeling too under the weather to be thinking straight?'

'I feel a bit better now that I've had something to eat.'

'And that would account for the suddenly relaxed body language?'

Becky didn't say anything but their eyes tangled and neither could look away—neither wanted to break the electric charge zapping between them. She could hear her breathing slowing up and could almost feel the rush of hot blood through her veins. Her skin prickled and her nipples were tightening, pinching, hard, throbbing buds poking against the flesh-coloured lace.

For Theo, things seemed to be happening in slow motion, from the darkening of her turquoise eyes to the raspy unsteadiness of his breathing.

His erection was a sheath of steel and would be outlined against his lightweight tan khakis. *Dip your eyes a bit lower, baby*, he thought, *and you'll have more than your fill of exactly how turned on I am right now.*

She did.

And that, too, seemed to happen in slow motion, as did the way the tip of her tongue erotically wetted her full lips. Her hair was everywhere, spread against the white pillows and over her shoulders, wild and tangled and utterly provocative.

'No sex,' he reminded her in a rough, shaky undertone and Becky looked at him, eyes lacking all guile as she considered what he had just pointed out.

'You stopped touching,' she heard herself say in a breathy voice—because suddenly it seemed very important for him to tell her that he still fancied her, even though she could read that he did in his eyes, and in the very still, controlled way he was standing. And in the erection he was not bothering to hide. She just needed him to say it…

'As per your instructions.'

'I know, but…'

'Are you fishing for me to tell you that I wanted to keep touching you? Because you won't have to throw your line very far to hear me say it. I wanted to keep touching you…' He raked his fingers through his hair. This was what he wanted and it was what he had wanted all along. When he thought about her body and what it could do to him, he had to suck his breath in sharply just to control his wayward libido from doing what it shouldn't. 'I wanted you after I left the Cotswolds and I haven't stopped. It's been hell looking and not being able to touch. Is that more or less what you wanted to hear…?'

Becky thought that she would like to hear much, much more. But *want* was all she was going to hear and she was sick of pretending to herself that she could keep pushing that aside because it didn't come with *love*.

She was too weak.

She had a few days left here and she was too weak to keep trying to be strong.

Whatever capacity Theo had to love, it was never going to be her. Privately, she didn't think he would ever love anyone.

'He never saw me in love,' his mother had whispered sadly to her only the evening before when he had been called away on one of the rare emergency conference calls he had allowed through. 'He just saw me when I was sad and alone. That's made him the man he is today. Afraid of love… Until now…until he found you…'

Becky had ignored the bit about Theo being afraid of love until he found her, which was a joke, and analysed and analysed and analysed the rest of what his mother had said. It might have been an over-simplification, but it was probably grounded in truth. His background had made him what he was when it came to love. He would never trust anything that had the power to destroy and, in his mind, his mother had been destroyed by love. He couldn't see beyond that and never would.

What he had to give and all he had to give was…his touch.

'More or less,' Becky agreed on a broken sigh. She pushed down the duvet, revealing the lacy nonsense she was wearing, which concealed nothing. Her pink nipples were visible through the lace, as was the shadowy dark down between her thighs.

She rested her hand on the mound between her legs, wanting badly to squeeze her legs together to relieve the fierce burning between them. His eyes were practically black with unconcealed lust and a heady sense of power raced through her veins, obliterating everything in its path.

'Becky.' Theo barely recognised his voice. 'There's something you should know…' All those half-truths were coming home to roost but she needed to know, needed to know that in life there was no such thing as coincidence, needed to know the truth about her cottage. What had seemed a good idea at the time, concealing the purpose of his arrival there so that he could feel out the terrain, was now an unthinkable error of judgement.

'Don't say a word,' Becky rushed in before he could say what she knew he was going to, another one of those warnings that what they were about to do was meaningless. She just didn't want to hear it. She didn't need to have that rammed home to her. Again.

'We have a few more days and after that we go our separate ways. We won't see one another again, so nothing has to be explained. We can…just enjoy this window…and then tomorrow is another day…'

CHAPTER NINE

HE WOULD TELL HER. Of course he would. Instead of being an anonymous buyer in three months' time, he would show his hand. He would also pay over the odds for the cottage he had originally intended to buy at a knock-down price, poetic justice for the people who had bought it at a knock-down price from his mother.

In three months' time, what they had now would all be water under the bridge. They'd probably chuckle as they exchanged contracts because, face it, she would have emerged a winner. She would be in a brand-new job in a brand-new location, renting a brand-new apartment. Work would have been done on the cottage so that the time left spent there would be comfortable. No buckets collecting water from a leaking roof!

She wasn't interested in hearing long stories now about his appearance at the cottage and the reasons behind it.

And he wasn't that interested in killing the moment by telling her either, although, in fairness, he would have done had she not waved aside his interruption.

She was fired up.

He was fired up.

Talk was just something taking up too much time when there was so much they both wanted to do.

Becky watched Theo's momentary flicker of hesitation and found that she was holding her breath. This was as proactive as she was capable of being. She knew that if he decided to back away now...if he thought that he wasn't prepared to step back into the water, even though she had assured him that these last few days would simply be about giving in to lust and closing that door between them once and for all...then she would retreat.

She would have lost her pride but, even so, she would retreat without regret because she was no longer prepared to turn her back on what could be hers for a few days more.

She was sick to the back teeth of being a noble martyr.

In the heat of the moment and with surrender in her mind, she couldn't, for the life of her, remember what had propelled her to fling down that 'no sex' addendum to the proposal he had put forward. She'd been so strident and sure of herself.

'You're not well,' Theo said gruffly.

'Why are you being so thoughtful?' Becky teased, not quite certain of the response she would get, but he grinned rakishly at her.

'Because I'm a gentleman.'

'Maybe I don't want you to be a gentleman right now,' Becky murmured, wriggling slightly to make room for him on the double bed. 'Are you sure you're not scared of getting into bed with me because you might catch my germs? I know you said that germs would never dare attack you but...'

'You're a witch.' Theo half-groaned. He walked towards the window and drew the curtains, plunging the room into instant darkness. He had to adjust his trousers, had to control his erection, which was throbbing under the zipper. He took a few seconds to stand by the window and look at her.

Very slowly he began undressing. This was more for his benefit than it was for hers. Move too fast and he would have to take her quick and hard, and he didn't want that. He wanted to enjoy every second of this—he wanted to savour her body and remember the feel of it under his exploring mouth and hands.

He wanted to take his time.

Becky fell back against the pillows as he began to stroll towards her. Shirt discarded, trousers unzipped. He was physical perfection. He was lean and muscular and looked *strong*. The sort of man who would always emerge the winner in any street brawl. She could have kept looking at him for ever.

She had no idea where her cold had gone. She had woken up feeling rotten, and thinking that she could do with a day off to recover from the impact daily contact with him was having on her state of mind, and now here she was, cold forgotten, as though it had never existed.

She was on fire but not with fever. She was burning up for the man now staring down at her, his hand resting lightly on his zipper. She could see the prominent bulge of his erection underneath the trousers. He was well endowed and he was massively turned on. It showed. It thrilled her.

She reached forward and lightly touched that bulge and the soft sound of his indrawn hiss was as powerful as any drug, sending her already drugged senses into frantic overdrive.

She sat up while he remained standing next to the bed.

The duvet had been shrugged off. Theo looked down at her soft shoulders, her riotous hair and all the luscious places exposed by the very revealing, and for her very risqué, nightwear. He greedily took in the heaviness of her breasts, lovingly outlined by the lace, two shades of flesh combined, her flesh and the flesh-coloured fabric. The deep crease of her cleavage made him grind his teeth together and he had to clench his fists to avoid pressing her back against the pillows so that he could ravish her.

And now she was gently but firmly pulling down the zipper and tugging the trousers down.

'Becky…' He groaned.

'I like it when you lose control…' she said in a ragged voice. He had stepped out of the trousers and she knew that he was having to restrain himself from pushing her back against the mattress so that he could do what came so naturally for him, so that he could take control of the situation.

No way.

She tugged down the boxers and circled her fingers firmly around his massive erection. She felt it pulse and then she delicately began to lick it from the head, along the thick shaft, trailing wetness up and down and around until he couldn't contain his groans. His hand was tangled in her hair. He wanted to keep her right there, doing what she was doing, even though, at the same time, he also wanted to tug her away so that she could stop taking him to that point of no return.

She took him into her mouth, sucking gently, then firmly, then back to gently, building a rhythm that was exciting her as much as it was exciting him. He was groaning, urging her on, telling her how he liked it. Before she'd met him, she would never have thought that she could be this intimate with a man, intimate enough to taste him like this. She'd never thought that she would be able to hear him say the sort of things Theo said to her in the height of their lovemaking…telling her where to go, what to do, urging her to do the same…describing all the things he wanted to do to her until she was burning up and frantic with desire.

'Stop,' he ordered gruffly, but it was too late, as she pushed him over the edge.

It was the last thing he'd wanted. He'd wanted slow and thorough. But it just went to show the effect she had on him. He hadn't been able to stop himself and he cursed fluently under his breath as he came down from a mind-blowing orgasm.

'Shame on you,' he chided, settling onto the bed with her, depressing the mattress with his weight so that she slid towards him, her body pressed up hard against his nakedness. 'I wanted to take things easy...' He pushed some of her hair behind an ear and then nibbled her lobe, which sent little arrows of beautiful sensation zipping through her.

She squirmed and wriggled against him, then slid one thigh sinuously up along his leg, relieving some of the aching between her legs.

'Naughty girl,' he admonished softly, grinning. 'You know you're going to have to pay dearly for making me lose control like that, don't you?'

He'd missed this—missed it much more than he'd ever imagined possible. Having her here in bed with him made him feel...weirdly comfortable, as though the inevitable was happening, as though he was meant to be here, doing this.

Finishing business, he thought, shrugging off a suddenly uneasy feeling he couldn't quite define.

He smoothed her thigh with his hand. She was warm and he paused to ask her whether she was up to it.

'You took something for your cold, I'm assuming?'

'Since when are you a fussing mother hen?' Becky laughed and leaned up to kiss him. His lips were firm and cool and so, so familiar. It amazed her how readily her body could recall his.

For a second, just a second, Theo stilled, then the moment was lost as he curved his fingers under the lace, finding her breasts, cupping them, moving to tease her nipple between his fingers. He gently pushed her flat against the bed and levered himself into the most advantageous position for exploring her body.

He started with her mouth. She'd taken him over the edge, but he was building fast to another erection, and this time he was going to take her all the way…feeling her wrap herself around him.

He kissed her slowly, tracing her lips with his tongue, then tasting her the way a connoisseur might taste vintage wine. He gently smoothed her hair away from her face, kissed her eyes, the sides of her mouth, then her neck.

She arched back slightly and shivered as those delicate kisses wound their way along her neck and then across her shoulders.

Her staccato breathing sounded as loud as thunder in the quiet of the bedroom. It was all she could hear. It was louder than the gentle background whirring of the ceiling fan, which she had become accustomed to keeping on all night, and punctuated with small whimpers and little, gasping moans.

She was desperate to rip the lace nightwear off but he wouldn't let her. Instead, he traced his tongue over the fabric, inexorably finding her nipple and then suckling hard on it through the lace, rasping it with his tongue until he found a gap in the lace through which it peeped, dusky pink, a hard button standing to attention.

'You're going to wreck this brand-new top,' she rebuked with a breathless giggle as she watched him toy with the intricate lace pattern until he had engineered two slightly bigger gaps, which he proceeded to position expertly over her nipples so that they were now both poking through.

'You shouldn't have bought it,' he countered, glancing at her and meeting her fevered eyes. 'You should have stuck to the baggy cotton tee shirts, then you wouldn't mind if I ripped it to shreds to get to your delectable body.'

'I was only obeying orders and replacing my wardrobe, as per your request...'

'Since when do you ever obey orders?' Theo asked huskily. 'You're the most disobedient mistress I've ever had.'

'I'm not your mistress!'

'You prefer "lover"?'

'I'd prefer you to stop talking.' *Wife*, she thought. She'd prefer *wife*. But *lover* would do, just as these snatched few days and nights would also have to do.

'Happy to oblige.' Theo took his time at her breasts. He sucked her nipples, giving them both the attention they deserved. He liked the way they stuck out at him through the lace, perfect, pouting and slickly wet from his tongue. He was almost reluctant to lift the top higher, to free them from their constraints, but he wanted to hold them in his hands. He had big hands and her breasts filled them, heavy and sexy. He massaged them and she writhed as he did so, tossing and turning, her eyes drowsy and unfocused with lust.

This was how he liked her. It startled him to realise that he had pictured this almost from the very moment he had left the cottage, having been marooned there by the snow. He hadn't just had her on his mind. He'd stored all sorts of images of her and projected them into a place and time where they would be doing just what they were doing now. Making love.

He nuzzled the undersides of her breasts, then trailed languid kisses along her stomach. Her skin was as soft and as smooth as satin. He paused at the indentation of her belly button, explored it with his tongue and heard her tell him that she needed him, that she was burning up for him. Her legs were already parted and he could smell the sweet, musky scent of her femininity.

She was breathing fast, panting, her stomach rising and falling as if she were running a marathon.

He cupped her between her legs and felt her wetness through the lace shorts, then he slipped his hand underneath and ran his finger along the tender, sensitive slit of her womanhood, finding and feeling her pulsing core.

The lace shorts restricted movement of his hand and he moved the barrier to one side. In a minute, he would take off the damned things completely, but right now he was enjoying watching her face as she responded to the gentle probing and teasing of his fingers.

Her eyelids fluttered, her nostrils were flared and her mouth was half-open. Her breathing was raspy and uneven, halfway between moaning and whimpering.

She was the very picture of a woman at the mercy of her body's physical responses and he felt a kick of satisfaction that he was the one who had brought her to that place. She might make a big song and dance about his unsuitability but she couldn't deny how much he turned her on.

Which was probably why his mother had not questioned their relationship. Normally so perceptive, Marita Rushing had not doubted for an instant that they were seriously involved. Yes, she might have wanted to believe it, and so had avoided gazing too closely for discrepancies in the perfect picture on display, but something about their interaction had convinced her that they were truly an item. Theo could only ascribe that to the physical pull between them which had transmitted itself to his mother by some sort of osmosis, making the pretence very, very real.

'You have no idea how much you turn me on,' he breathed in a rough undertone and Becky looked at him with darkened eyes.

'You could try telling me. I need convincing after you've spent so long ignoring me...'

'I like to think of it as a slow burn...' He eased the shorts off and she half-sat up, tugged the top over her head and flung it to the ground, then lay back, propping herself against the pillows.

Theo paused, taking time out to look at her, so supple and soft and so very, very feminine. The height of femininity, with her rounded curves, her long hair and open, honest face.

He straddled her and then knelt, his legs on either side of her, so that he could continue his lazy exploration of her glorious body. He had to keep telling himself not to rush because he wanted to, badly. He had to make himself slow down, although it was nigh on impossible when he moved down her body and began to lick her between her legs, tasting her, savouring her dewy wetness in his mouth. He nudged his erection into some good behaviour because there was no way he was going to allow himself to lose control again. Once had been bad enough.

Becky could barely breathe. It was exquisite having him down there, head between her legs, his hands under her bottom, driving her up to his mouth so that not even the slightest fraction of sensation was lost.

She hooked her legs around his back and flattened

her hands at her sides. She could feel the steady rhythm of an orgasm building and eased away from his mouth, panting, not wanting to come, wanting and needing him inside her.

Theo straightened, lying lightly over her so that he could deliver a few little kisses to her mouth. 'You have no idea how long I've wanted this,' he confessed unsteadily. He pushed himself up and Becky traced the corded muscles of his arms.

'How long?' Becky made her voice light, teasing and mildly amused. She hoped that only she could hear the desperate plea to have something, *anything* to grab on to, that would turn this into more than just sex for him. It would never be love or anything like that, but affection, maybe... Would that be asking too much? She was only human, after all.

'Pretty much as soon as I stepped out of your front door.' He dealt her a slashing, wicked grin that made her toes curl.

'You could have stayed a little longer.'

'Unfortunately...' Theo nuzzled the side of her neck so that some of what he was saying was lost in the caress '...there was a certain little something called *reality* to be dealt with. Playing truant can only last so long...'

'A bit like what we're doing here.' Becky laughed lightly, although her heart was constricted with pain.

'This is a bit more than truancy.' Theo looked down at her seriously. 'It's not just about having some fun and then pushing on. There's someone else in the equation.'

'But essentially it *is* just fun and pushing on. I mean, we're here and we're in bed together, and then we'll leave and that'll be that...'

Theo shrugged. He wasn't going to cross any bridges until he was staring them in the face. 'I plan on bringing my mother back as soon as possible,' he admitted. 'It's all very well and good, her being out here—and I'm sure she's enjoying the weather, my aunt's company and my aunt's kids and grandchildren—but that's a form of truancy in itself, wouldn't you agree?'

'Maybe...'

'And, as for us pushing on... I admit things are slightly more complex on that front than I'd originally imagined.'

'How so?' Becky felt her racing heart begin to stutter. Tense as a bow string, she waited for him to elucidate.

'All this talk is killing the mood.' Theo shifted to turn onto his side and pulled her into position so that they were facing one another, belly to belly. 'I thought my mother would have been delighted to discover that I was capable of more than having flimsy relationships with unsuitable women. I imagined that that would have given her a fillip, so to speak. Bucked up her spirits and stopped her from having worst-case scenarios in her head about me remaining a bachelor for the rest of my days, because somehow I was incapable of forming bonds with any woman that might be permanent. I intended to insinuate that you might not be the one for me, but certainly there was a woman out there who would be...a woman who wasn't a supermodel with nothing much between her ears...'

'Not all models are like that.' Becky thought of her clever, lovely sister.

'I know,' Theo admitted. 'But maybe I've just made it my mission to find the ones who are. At any rate, I was perhaps a bit short-sighted. I also thought that I'd be able to break things off between us gently. A process of gradually growing apart because of the distance or my work commitments or your work commitments. No need for you to put in an appearance—just a slow and gradual demise which could be explained away without any visits from you. I had no idea that my mother would jump on board this charade with such rich enthusiasm or that she would...' he sighed and searched for the right words, and then shot her a crooked, sideways smile '...fall in love with you the way she has. It poses a problem, although it's not something we can't work with.'

'What problem?'

'It'll wait. I can't talk any more, Becky...' He dipped his fingers into her and slid them up and down. 'And neither can you, from the feel of things.'

He didn't give her time to pick up the threads of the conversation or even to dwell further on it, because he lowered himself down the length of her agitated body, hands on her sides, mouth kissing, licking and nibbling.

She gave a husky groan as he buried his head between her legs again, teasing with the same lingering thoroughness as he had earlier teased her tight, sensitive nipples. She curled her fingers into his hair, arched back and bucked in gentle, rotating movements, urging on his inquisitive tongue to taste every bit of her.

Her body was on fire and she feverishly played with her nipples, driving yet more sensation through her body. She was so close to coming...

But, when she could stand it no more, he reared up and rustled about, finding protection, giving her body a little time to breathe and for those almost-there sensations to subside.

She couldn't wait to have him inside her. Like him, she hadn't stopped wanting this. Unlike him, so much more was attached to her wanting, but for the moment she couldn't even begin to go down that road, not when she was burning up.

He inserted himself gently into her. He was big and

every time they had made love he had been careful to build his rhythm slowly, had eased himself slowly into her, before thrusting deeper and firmer.

She loved the feel of him in her, loved it when he began to move with surety and precision, knowing just how to rouse her, just where to touch her and when for maximum effect. It was as though her body had been groomed to respond to him in ways that she knew, in her heart, it would never, ever respond to any other man.

And this time it was no different. He pushed deep and hard and she automatically bent her knees, taking all of him inside her and feeling the rush of her orgasm as it hurtled towards her, sending her to a place where nothing existed but the sound of their breathing and movement, and then a splintering that was so intense that the world seemed to freeze completely.

Distantly, she knew that he was coming as well, felt the tension in his big body as he reared up with a strangled groan of completion and satisfaction.

She wrapped her arms around him, her eyes still closed and her breathing still laboured, shuddering as she came down from the high to which she had been catapulted. He stayed still for a while, his arms encasing her. It was such an illusion of absolute closeness that she wanted to cry.

Instead, she whispered softly, stroking his face until he opened his eyes and looked at her. 'You were telling me that there's a problem, Theo...'

'Isn't it usually the unthinking man who breaks the post-coital mood by talking? Or falling asleep? Or getting up to work?' Theo half-joked, kissing the tip of her nose.

'I wonder which of those three would be your preferred choice of atmosphere-breaking?' Becky darted a kiss on his mouth, which deepened into something more intense.

'With you...' Theo murmured, cupping her breast and absently playing with her nipple, rolling the pad of his thumb over it, thinking that he could easily dip down to suckle on it and just stay there until they were both ready to make love all over again, which, judging from the way his penis was behaving, would be sooner rather than later. 'With you, I could happily go for the repeat performance option...'

'Not yet.'

Theo flopped onto his back and laughed ruefully. 'Okay. Here's the problem.' He sighed and took a few seconds to get his brain back into gear before shifting onto his side to look at her. 'I don't think it's going to be easy for you to simply vanish from my life overnight, whilst I paper over your disappearance with as many limp excuses as I can think of. My mother may have had her spirit sapped by her ill health and worries but she's still vigorous enough to do something like demand a meeting with you to find out why we aren't making wedding plans. I asked you for a fortnight. It might not be long enough.'

'It has to be, Theo. I have a life to be getting on with.' She pushed herself away from him and then kept her hand flat on his chest to stop him from coming any closer.

'I get that.' Did he? Honestly? He didn't think that a few more days of this was going to be nearly enough to get her out of his system.

'I'm not going to be at your beck and call just because you think you might need me to put in an occasional appearance.'

'What about being at my beck and call because I can't seem to keep my hands off you and I don't want you to disappear from my life?'

If he hadn't said that…

If he'd just let her keep thinking that all he wanted was a continuation of the business arrangement they had embarked upon…

He didn't want her to disappear from his life. She knew that it was silly to read anything behind that but her romantic heart couldn't help but be swept away by the notion of fate having brought them together, delivered them to this place, this here and now, where possibilities were endless, if only he could see it.

'I know you don't mean that,' she muttered, confused and hearing the uncertainty in her voice with some alarm.

'I've never meant anything more in my life before, Becky,' Theo told her with driven urgency. He could sense her capitulation but he didn't feel the expected triumph. Instead, he felt a rush of heartfelt honesty that took him by surprise. This wasn't just about his mother. Oh, no…this was about *him*. She was a fever inside him and he knew that just a little bit longer with her would douse it. Overpowering *need* had never cut so deep.

'It's not practical, Theo, and besides…'

'Besides what…?' She didn't answer and he looked at her with deadly seriousness. 'Tell me you don't feel this too, Becky. This has nothing to do with my mother. I would be asking this of you were my mother not a factor in the equation. I don't want to let you go…'

Just yet, Becky reminded herself, clutching at sanity the way a drowning man clutched at a life raft. *You don't want to let me go just yet…*

She couldn't afford to let herself be lured any further along the road than she already had been. She was in love with him. Each day spent with him was a day deeper in love for her. She had cracked this time, had argued herself into a position of being able to justify her surrender.

So was she going to do that again? Until she was finally dispatched at some point in the not-too-distant future?

Theo knew that this was not only a tall order but an extremely rash one. It would be difficult to write her out of his life abruptly, but it could be done. There were always ways and means when it came to solving thorny problems. But he still really wanted her, and wanted her so badly that the need took precedence over clear judgement.

He was involved with her because of the cottage. Break up with her when they returned to England, and he could still buy the place after the dust had settled. They would have had a few sex-filled days in the Cotswolds and a dalliance in the sun generated from the extraordinary circumstance that had brought them together.

Continue, for whatever reason, when they returned to London, and like it or not they would be indulging in a full-blown relationship. What else could he possibly call it? Whatever she said about him not being her type, how long before that would change? Would she inevitably be seduced by a lifestyle she had never envisaged for herself? Once upon a time, he had doubted that she would fit in to his world, not that he'd really given a damn. He'd been wrong. Looking at the ease with which she'd pulled off the expensive couture clothes she had bought, he realised she fitted in just fine.

Haute couture was something a woman could get accustomed to very easily. How long, then, before she became just another woman trying to talk about marriage and planning things that would never materialise?

But none of that seemed to matter because the sex was just so good.

And anyway, he argued with himself, he would have *some* contact with her afterwards because of the practice he had promised to buy for her. He would have to have her input in sourcing somewhere suitable. It wasn't as though they could just walk away from one another without a backward glance.

There and then, he made his decision. The purchase of the cottage would have to be jettisoned. That had been an error of judgement, given everything that had come afterwards, and she would never find out about any of it. At any rate, Becky would soon be busy changing jobs and facing the challenges of living somewhere else. They would see one another but not regularly. His mother might see her again a few times but that would be it. Harmless dinners out where he would be able to manage the conversation.

It would be a shame about the cottage, but you won a few, you lost a few.

He slipped his hand between her legs and kissed her, a long, lingering, persuasive kiss. This was what he knew, the power of sex, and he was going to force her to admit to it too. He wasn't going to let her walk away in a haze of high-principled apologies and rambling, earnest lectures about what made sense and what didn't. If she walked away, then she was going to face what she was walking away from. Explosive, mind-blowing sex.

It was hitting below the belt, but Theo was nothing if not a man who knew how to take advantage of the situations life threw at him.

Becky moaned, her whole body quivering as he began devastating inroads into her self-control. He moved his fingers and touched her until she wanted to scream and beg him to take her. Her mind slipped its leash and she imagined all sorts of things she wanted him to do to her. She imagined what it would be like to pin down those powerful arms of his, restrain them with a nice leather strap and then torment his body by making love to him oh, so slowly…

She imagined them naked in a field making love under a black, starry sky, and touching one another in the back row of a cinema like a couple of teenagers…

And then the slideshow ended because none of that would happen if she walked away now.

She didn't want any of that to happen. She knew the consequences of prolonging this disastrous union.

But she still reached down anyway, held his erection in her slight hand and began massaging it before climbing on top of him and letting herself surrender…

CHAPTER TEN

HOW COULD YOU...? How could you do this...?

Ten days ago, that was exactly what Becky had wanted to scream and shout at the man who once again had become her lover, against her better judgement.

She had thought at the time that being bedridden for a day with a cold virus would give her breathing space. In fact, as it had turned out, being bedridden had placed her in just the right place for him to stage his very successful assault on what precious little had been left of her common sense.

She'd folded faster than the speed of light and they had spent the remainder of their stay in Italy unable to keep their hands off one another. Much to his mother's obvious delight.

And, after they had returned to England, she had kept telling herself that it was just a matter of time before it all fizzled out. That work commitments and all the details that had to be sorted out with her job and the new practice would reduce their time together until they simply drifted apart though lack of proximity. He wasn't the sort of man who could ever do a long-distance relationship or indeed any relationship where the woman he wanted was inaccessible.

Certainly, she had had to return to the Cotswolds, had

had to begin the process of dismantling her life there and beginning the search for somewhere new where a practice could be profitable. Yet, somehow, she seemed to have seen him over the ensuing fortnight with more regularity than she might have imagined, and then his mother had returned from Italy, earlier than he had anticipated.

Becky stared numbly around her, back where she had started at the cottage, which had now been renovated to a standard that was eminently saleable.

In fact, she barely recognised the place.

She blinked rapidly, squashing foolish tears at her own naivety. There was no such thing as a free lunch and especially not in the rarefied world that Theo occupied.

At the time, she had thought, unwisely, that the cottage and the practice were part of the deal that he had hired her to undertake. Play the game and she would be rewarded—and she had played the game, not for the rewards, but for the pleasure of playing because she had missed him. He had phoned and she had got herself in a lather and called upon her pride but, in the end, she had thrilled at the thought of just seeing him again and being with him again.

But, of course, the picture was a lot more complex than the one that had been painted for her benefit.

She paused to gaze at herself in the mirror in the newly painted hall. She'd dumped all the finery, the expensive dresses, the designer shoes and underwear.

This is who you are, she told her reflection. *A pleasant enough looking vet who's lived her entire life in the country. Not some glamorous sex kitten powerful enough to turn the head of a man like Theo Rushing.*

What on earth had got into her?

She knew, of course. Love had got into her. It had roared into her life and she had been knocked off her feet without even realising it because it had come in a format she hadn't recognised.

She'd expected someone like Freddy. She'd expected cuddles, kisses and, face it, polite, enjoyable sex.

She hadn't expected sex of the bodice-ripping variety, so she had written it off as lust until, of course, it had all been far too late for her adequately to protect herself.

Love had turned her into a puppet that had walked back into his arms, even though she had known that it was never going to be reciprocated. Love had effectively switched off all the burglar alarms that should have been up and running, protecting her.

And, disastrously, love had made her begin to hope.

She'd begun to think that he might just feel more for her than he had anticipated. People said one thing, but life had a way of getting in the way of all their well-grounded intentions.

Look at her!

Had it been the same for him? It surely wasn't just about the sex…? There'd been many times when they hadn't been rolling around on a bed, when they'd talked, when he'd given her advice on setting up a practice— brilliant, sensible advice from a guy who had done his own thing and come out on top.

It hadn't been the same for him. He'd had an agenda from the word *go* and, oh, how she had wanted to scream and shout when she had found out. Instead, she had absented herself and taken off to France for a week to be with her family, who had been overjoyed to see her.

For a while, she had almost been distracted enough to see a way forward. She had revelled in her sister's pregnancy and obvious happiness. She had allowed herself to be congratulated on her ambitions to move on and set up a practice while she had skirted around the precise explanation as to how, exactly, she was managing to do that. She had waffled a lot about excellent references, possible bank loans and the possibility of someone willing to invest for a share of the partnership...

Now she was back, though...

She peered through the window in the hall by the front door.

For the first time in ten days, ever since she had found out from his mother details of his past which he had conveniently kept from her, she would be seeing him.

She had no idea what was going through his head but she hadn't wanted him to know what had been going through hers. At least not then, not when she had been so boiling mad, so humiliated and mortified, that her emotions would have done the shouting and that would have made her incoherent and vulnerable.

And, when she confronted him, she wanted to be cool and detached.

She also wasn't even certain that she would mention anything at all. Perhaps she would just tell him that she felt that what they had had run its course. Maybe he had got the hint, because she hadn't been returning his calls, and on the couple of occasions when he had managed to get through to her she had been vague and distant, practically ending the conversation before it had begun.

She ducked away from the window the second she heard the throaty purr of his car and the crunch of gravel as it swerved into the little courtyard in front of the house.

Nerves gripped her. The doorbell sounded and she wiped her perspiring palms on her jeans and took a deep breath.

Experience told her that, when she pulled open the door, his impact on her would be as strong as it always was. Absence and time apart were two things that never seemed to diminish it. Unless he had gained two stone in the space of ten days and lost all his hair and teeth, his devastating good looks would still make the breath hitch in her throat and the flood of emotion she felt for him would still make her feel weak and powerless.

Not wanting to appear over-keen, she allowed him to stand pressing the doorbell for a few seconds before she opened the door.

And there he was.

The weather had changed from those heady few days when he had last been in the Cotswolds. Spring had long since arrived, and with it pale blue skies and wispy clouds were scurrying across the washed blue backdrop as though hurrying on urgent errands. The trees were in full bloom and the flowers were poking out wherever they could, eager to feel the first rays of sun on them, blues and violets and reds and pinks clambering out of the bushes and hedgerows and tumbling across fences and yellow stone walls.

It was Saturday. No work, hence his arrival at four in the afternoon, just a few hours after she herself had arrived back from France. He was long and lean in faded black jeans and a black polo shirt, casual jacket hooked over one shoulder. He'd propped his shades up and he looked every inch a drop-dead-sexy movie star.

And she felt all those predictable responses she always did whenever she clapped eyes on him.

'Theo,' she managed, stepping aside and then slightly back as he brushed past her.

His clean, woody scent filled her nostrils and made her feel faint.

'So…' Theo turned to look at her. His face was impassive. His body language was cool and controlled. Neither bore any resemblance to what was going on inside him because she'd spent the past ten days playing an avoidance game that had got on his nerves. She'd vanished off to France on a whim. She'd contrived to view possible practices up for grabs without him, even though he was going to be funding whatever purchase transpired.

'What's going on, Becky?'

They hadn't made it out of the narrow hall and already it was clear there were going to be no pleasantries to paper over the awkwardness of what she was going to say. Ending something was always tough but she was going to be ending this with an edge of bitterness that would live with her for ever, and that made it all the tougher.

'I thought I would show you the practice I'm thinking would be suitable. The head vet who runs it is retiring and he's looking for someone to take over. It'll be a similar sort of size to the one here and, if anything, the work will be less demanding and probably a lot more profitable because it's in a town.' She began edging towards the sitting room.

Two weeks ago, she would have flown into his arms and they wouldn't have made it to the bedroom.

If he hadn't got the message already that things were over between them, then he'd have to be blind not to be receiving the message loud and clear now. And he wasn't blind. Far from it.

'I know buying the practice was all…er…part of the deal that we had…'

Theo stayed her with one hand and spun her round to face him. 'This is how you greet me after nearly two weeks of absence, Becky?' He stepped closer towards her, a forbidding, towering presence that filled her with apprehension, nerves and that tingling excitement that was now taboo. 'With polite conversation about business deals?'

She whipped her arm away and stepped back, anger rising like a tide of bile at the back of her throat.

'Okay,' she snapped, reaching boiling point at the speed of light. 'How else would you like me to greet you? You must have guessed that…that…' She faltered, and he stepped into the sudden leaden silence like a predator sensing weakness.

'That…? Why don't you spell it out for me, Becky?'

'It's over. I…I'm moving on now and it's time for this to end.' She looked away because she just couldn't look at him. She could feel his grey eyes boring into her, trying to pull thoughts out of her head.

He knew. How could he not? One minute she had been full on and the next minute she had left the building. He'd tried to get in touch with her, and, sure, she'd picked up a few times, but conversation between them had been brief and stilted. He would have called a lot more because her silence had driven him crazy but pride, again, had intervened.

He felt sick. What was it they said about pride being a person's downfall? Except it had always been so much part and parcel of his personality. He wanted nothing more now than to shrug his shoulders and walk away. Let his lawyers deal with whatever had to be done in connection with the practice, sort out whatever paperwork needed sorting out.

He couldn't and he was afflicted by something alien to him. A wave of desperation.

He needed to move so he headed for the kitchen, barely glancing at the renovations his money had paid for. She was saying something from behind him, something about paying back whatever money he lent her. He spun around and cut her short with a slice of his hand,

'Why?' he grated savagely. 'And you can drop the

"time to move on" act. The last time we saw one another you were wriggling like an eel under me and begging me to take you.'

Becky went bright red. Trust him to bring sex into it—trust him to use it as a lever in his line of reasoning—yet why should she be surprised when it was the only thing that motivated him? That and the cool detachment that could allow him to see manipulation as something acceptable.

She moved to stand by the sink, pressed up against it with her hands behind her back because she was too restless to sit at the kitchen table.

'Maybe,' she burst out on a wave of uncontrolled anger that was heavily laced with fury at herself for ever, ever having thought that he might actually have proper feelings for her, 'it's because I've finally decided that having a bastard in my life is something I can do without!'

Theo went completely still. For once, his clever mind that could be relied upon to deal with any situation had stalled and was no longer functioning.

Their eyes met and she was the first to look away. Even in the grip of anger, he still exerted the sort of power over her that made her fearful because she knew how out of character it could make her behave.

'Explain.' He felt cold inside because he knew what she was going to say and, in retrospect, marvelled that he had ever thought that she wouldn't find out, marvelled that he had ever felt he could carry on having this relationship and then walk away from it with her none the wiser.

'You didn't just *happen to come here* while you were out taking your car for a little spin in the middle of nowhere, did you, Theo?' She had regained some of her self-control and her voice was low, but steady.

'You weren't just the *poor marooned billionaire* unfortunate enough to wash up on the doorstep of a country bumpkin with a house falling down around her ears, were you? You came here because you wanted to buy the place. Your mother told me. She told me how much she'd been hankering to return to the house where she and your father had lived as a young couple. She told me how she'd left in a hurry after he'd been killed in a road accident. She said that she'd never wanted to return but that lately she'd been wanting to make peace with her past and especially now that you seemed to be so happy and settled.' She laughed scornfully but her cheeks were bright red and her hands were shaking. 'When did you decide that it made more sense to check out the place and see for yourself how much it was worth? When did you decide that you would sleep with me so that it would be easier to talk me into selling it for the lowest possible price? The power of pillow talk and all that? Did you decide to put your little plan on hold temporarily because using me as a fake girlfriend was more important than yanking the house out from under my feet?

'After all, you'd already slept with me—why not keep it up for a few more weeks until your mother was over her little turn? Then a clean break-up and a speedy purchase! You'd already done the groundwork to get the place up to your standards. Were you ever going to tell me that you were behind the purchase? Or were you going to string me along for a while longer, until you got me to the point where you could convince me to sell it for a song before regrettably letting me go, like all those women you dated before me?'

Theo raked his fingers through his hair.

Consequences he had put on hold were ramming into him with the force of a runaway steam engine and fact was so intricately weaved with conjecture that he was well and truly on the back foot.

But that didn't bother him. What bothered him was that he had blown it.

He'd blown the only good thing to have happened in his life with his arrogance, his misplaced pride and his driving need to exert control over everything.

'Let me explain,' he said roughly, which provoked another bitter laugh, and he couldn't blame her. He couldn't have sounded more guilty of the accusations hurled at him if he'd tried.

'I don't want you to explain!'

'Why did you let me drive here if you didn't want to hear what I had to say?' he countered in a driven voice. He badly wanted to get closer to her, to close the distance between them, but it would be a big mistake. For once, words were going to have to be his allies. For once, he was going to have to say how he felt, and that scared him. He'd never done it before and now...

She hated him. It was written all over her face. But she hadn't, not before. No, she might have protested that he wasn't her type, but they'd clicked in a way he'd never clicked with a woman before.

He should have told her the truth when he'd had the chance in Portofino. He'd started but had allowed himself to be side-tracked. Now, he was paying a price he didn't want to pay.

'You're right. I did come here with the sole intention of buying this place. My mother had been making noises about wanting to return here. I had the money and I saw no reason not to take back what, I felt, had been taken from her at a knockdown price.' He held up his hand because he could see her bursting to jump in and, if nothing else, he would have his say. He had to. He had no choice.

'You used me.'

'I exploited a situation and at the time it felt like the right thing to do.' He looked at her with searing honesty and she squashed all pangs of empathy. 'I don't like having this conversation with you standing there. Won't you come here?'

'I don't like thinking that you used me. So that makes both of us not liking things that aren't about to change.'

Come nearer? Did anyone ever take up an invitation to jump into a snake pit?

And still her body keened for him in a way that was positively terrifying.

'Sleeping with me was all just part of your plan, wasn't it?'

'I would never have slept with you if I didn't fancy you, Becky. And fancy you more than I've ever fancied any woman in my life before. Okay, so you might think that what I did was unethical, but—'

'But?' She tilted her head to one side in a polite enquiry. At least he'd fancied her. He wasn't lying. That, in itself, was a comfort. *Small comfort*, she quickly reminded herself.

'But it was the only way I knew how to be,' he said in such a low, husky voice that she had to strain to hear him.

Unsettled, she felt herself relax a little, although she remained where she was, pressed against the counter, careful not to get too close. And she wasn't going to ask him what he meant either!

But her keen eyes noted the way he angled his big body so that he was leaning towards her, head lowered, arms resting on his thighs and his hands clasped loosely together. That looked like defeat in his posture, although she was probably wildly off the mark with that one. She seemed to have turned being wildly off the mark into a habit as far as this man was concerned.

Theo dealt her a hesitant glance.

He had such beautiful eyes, she thought, shaken by that hesitancy, such wildly extravagant eyelashes, and when he looked like that, as though he was searching in fog to find a way forward, was it any wonder that something inside her wasn't quite as steely as it should be?

'I've always been tough,' he admitted in the same low, barely audible voice and she took a couple of tentative steps towards him, then sat at the table, but at the opposite end. Theo glanced across and wondered if he dared let his hopes rise, considering she was no longer pressed against the counter like a cornered rat preparing to attack. 'I've had to be. Life wasn't easy when I was growing up, but I think I told you that.'

'Whilst omitting to tell me other things,' Becky pointed out with asperity, although her voice wasn't as belligerent as it had previously been.

'Granted.' He hung his head for a few seconds, then held her eyes once again. 'My mother was always unhappy. Not that she wasn't a good mother—she was a great mother—but she'd never recovered from my father's death. Love cut short in its prime will always occupy top position on the pedestal.' He shot her a crooked smile. 'She got very little for the cottage in the end. She sold low and, by the time the mortgage was paid off, she barely had enough to buy something else. She had to work her fingers to the bone to make sure we had food in the larder and heating during winter. That was what I saw and that was what, I guess, made me realise that love and emotion were weaknesses to be avoided at all costs. What mattered was security and only money could give you that. I locked my heart away and threw away the key. I was invincible. It never occurred to me that I wouldn't have to find the key to open it because someone else would do that for me.'

Becky felt prickles of something speckle her skin. She took a deep breath and held it.

'It made financial sense to buy the cottage cheap. My plan was to go there, fling money on the table and take what should have been my mother's as far as I was concerned. But then you opened the door and things changed—and then we slept together and after that everything kept changing. I kept telling myself that nothing had, that I was still going to buy the cottage, but I was in freefall without even realising it. Becky, I wanted to tell you why I'd shown up on your doorstep, but I'd boxed myself in and I couldn't get a grip to manoeuvre myself out.'

He shook his head ruefully. She was so still and for once he couldn't read what she was thinking. It didn't matter. He had to plough on anyway.

'In the end, I wasn't going to buy it,' he confessed heavily. 'I'd made that decision before we returned to this country. The only problem was that I never followed through with the reasoning because, if I had, I would have realised that the reason I dumped the plan to buy your house for my mother was because I'd fallen in love with you, and to do anything as underhand as try and buy you out, even if you agreed to sell, would have felt… somehow wrong.'

'You what? Say that again? I think…I think I must have missed something…'

'I've been an idiot.' Theo looked at her steadily. 'And I don't know how long I would have carried on being an idiot. I just know that the past ten days have been hell and, when you told me that you wanted me out of your life just now, my world felt like it was collapsing.

Becky…' He searched to find the words for a role he had never played before. 'I realise you don't consider me the ideal catch…'

'Stop.' Her head was buzzing from hearing stuff she'd never in a million years thought she'd ever hear. She was on cloud nine and now the distance between them seemed too great when all she wanted was to be able to reach out and touch him. She saw the shadow of defeat cross his face and her heart constricted.

'I *did* think that you weren't the sort of guy for me. I'd always made assumptions about the sort of guy who *would* be for me and you didn't fit the bill. There was so much about you that I'd never come across in my life before.' She smiled, eyes distant as she recalled those first impressions when he'd appeared on her doorstep in all his drop-dead, show-stopping glory. 'But you were irresistible,' she confessed. 'And it wasn't just about the way you looked, although it was easier for me to tell myself that. Everything about you was irresistible. I was hooked before I even went to bed with you, and then you disappeared without a backward glance.'

'Not so,' Theo murmured. 'If only you knew.' He patted his lap and she obediently and happily went to sit there. She sighed with pleasure because this was where she belonged. Close to him. If this turned out to be a dream, she was hoping not to wake any time soon.

'When you got in touch, I was so excited, then I realised that you'd only got in touch because you wanted something from me. That I was the only woman who could deliver that something, because I was plain and average and the sort of girl boys don't mind taking home to their mothers.'

'You're the sexiest woman I've ever known,' he assured her with a seriousness that made her smile again.

'The bonus is that you're also the type of woman I was proud to introduce to my mother.'

'I put down that "no sex" clause,' Becky said thoughtfully, 'but I was still excited to be seeing you again. Through it all, even when I was so angry—because some of the things you said, like me having to buy a whole new wardrobe to be a convincing girlfriend, were really offensive—I was still excited. It was like I could suddenly only come alive in your company.' She sighed. 'Which brings us right back to where we started. With the cottage and your reasons for showing up.'

'I think there's something my mother wants a lot more than a cottage.' He dropped a kiss on the side of her mouth and then, as she curved into him, looping her arms around his neck, the kiss deepened and deepened until he was in danger of forgetting what he wanted to say. Eventually he drew back and looked at her. 'She wants a daughter-in-law and I've realised that there's nothing more I want, my darling, than a wife. So…will you marry me?'

'You called me your darling…'

'And will you let me call you my *wife*?'

'My darling husband-to-be… Yes, I will.

* * * * *

If you enjoyed this story, check out these other great reads from Cathy Williams:
A VIRGIN FOR VASQUEZ
SEDUCED INTO HER BOSS'S SERVICE
WEARING THE DE ANGELIS RING
THE SURPRISE DE ANGELIS BABY
THE WEDDING NIGHT DEBT
Available now!

MILLS & BOON®

MODERN™

POWER, PASSION AND IRRESISTIBLE TEMPTATION

MILLS & BOON®

EXCLUSIVE EXTRACT

Natalia Di Sione hasn't left the family estate in years,
but she must retrieve her grandfather's lost book of
poems from Angelos Menas! The lives of the brooding
Greek and his daughter were changed irrevocably by a
fire, and Talia finds herself drawn to the formidable
tycoon. She knows the untold pleasure Angelos offers is
limited, but when she leaves with the book, will her
heart remain behind on the island?

Read on for a sneak preview of
A DI SIONE FOR THE GREEK'S PLEASURE
by Kate Hewitt

"Talia…" Angelos's voice broke on her name, and then,
before she could even process what was happening, he pulled
her towards him, his hands hard on her shoulders as his
mouth crashed down on hers and plundered its soft depths.

It had been ten years since she'd been kissed, and then
only a schoolboy's brush. She'd never been kissed like this,
never felt every sense blaze to life, every nerve ending tingle
with awareness, nearly painful in its intensity, as Angelos's
mouth moved on hers and he pulled her tightly to him.

His hard contours collided against her softness, each
point of contact creating an unbearably exquisite ache of
longing as she tangled her hands in his hair and fit her
mouth against his.

She was a clumsy, inexpert kisser, not sure what to do
with her lips or tongue, only knowing that she wanted more
of this. Of him.

She felt his hand slide down to cup her breast, his palm

hot and hard through the thin material of her dress, and a gasp of surprise and delight escaped her.

That small sound of pleasure was enough to jolt Angelos out of his passion-fogged daze, for he dropped his hand and in one awful, abrupt movement tore his mouth from hers and stepped back.

"I'm sorry," he said, his voice coming out in a ragged gasp.

"No…" Talia pressed one shaky hand to her buzzing lips as she tried to blink the world back into focus. "Don't be sorry," she whispered. "It was wonderful."

"I shouldn't have—"

"Why not?" she challenged. She felt frantic with the desperate need to feel and taste him again, and more importantly, not to have him withdraw from her, not just physically, but emotionally. Angelos didn't answer and she forced herself to ask the question again. "Why not, Angelos?"

"Because you are my employee, and I was taking advantage of you," he gritted out. "It was not appropriate…"

"I don't care about appropriate," she cried. She knew she sounded desperate and even pathetic but she didn't care. She wanted him. She *needed* him. "I care about you," she confessed, her voice dropping to a choked whisper, and surprise and something worse flashed across Angelos's face. He shook his head, the movement almost violent and terribly final.

"No, Talia," he told her flatly. "You don't."

Don't miss
A DI SIONE FOR THE GREEK'S PLEASURE
by Kate Hewitt

Available December 2016